IN EVERY CLOUD

By the Author

Venus in Love

In Every Cloud

IN EVERY CLOUD

by

Tina Michele

2015

IN EVERY CLOUD

ISBN 13: 978-1-62639-413-1

This Trade Paperback Original Is Published By
Bold Strokes Books, Inc.
P.O. Box 249
Valley Falls, NY 12185

First Edition: August 2015

CREDITS
EDITOR: CINDY CRESAP
PRODUCTION DESIGN: STACIA SEAMAN
COVER DESIGN BY SHERI (GRAPHICARTIST2020@HOTMAIL.COM)

Acknowledgments

My love for North Carolina runs deep, as does my love for the wonderful family that showed me just how beautiful it all is. There isn't any part of that world I don't hold close to my heart. Forever and for always.

Thank you to my readers—Sarah, Angela, Kena, Holli, and Teresa. Thank you to my family for being just as weird and wonderful as ever. Words cannot describe how lucky I am to call you my own. Thank you to Cindy for teaching me more in the last year than I ever learned in school. And thank you to BSB for another amazing opportunity and for letting me be a part of this family.

II.XXIX.MM

CHAPTER ONE

Bree Whitley wandered through the empty rooms of the house. She looked behind doors and on windowsills while she waited for her uncle to answer his phone. Bree switched hers from one ear to the other and pushed back the shower curtain to take another look. After all, she might have missed something the first eighteen times she'd inspected the bathroom. "Hello?" Bree asked just in case she'd missed his hello in that split second. Instead of a voice, there was another ring. "Or not."

As she exited the bathroom, she heard a man's voice on the line. "Hey, Breezy. How are you, kiddo?"

Bree smiled at the term of endearment. It was a welcome comfort in her current mixed state of anxiety and sorrow. While her uncle had never treated her like a child, the childlike feeling of security she felt when he called her Breezy was always welcome. "Hi, Uncle Jim. I'm okay. I keep pacing around looking in the cracks and crevices for something that I may have forgotten." After a long pause, Bree whimpered, "Oh God, I don't know if I can do this." Bree felt the stinging burn of the tears that filled her eyes. She covered her mouth just in time to muffle a sob.

"I know it's hard, kiddo. But you said this was what you

needed. If you want to stay that's your choice, but do it because it's the best thing for *you*."

Bree backed up against the nearest wall and slid to the floor with a heavy thump. She stared at the ceiling and fought back the tears with all her might. "I know, but I just never thought my life wouldn't have her in it. She was the reason for everything I did. Without her, what's the point of anything?"

"Bree, sweetheart, you're a strong and beautiful woman. I know it feels like your world is falling in around you, but I promise it will get better, my love. Come home. Before you know it, you'll be happy again."

Home. Bree thought she was home—a beautiful home with a beautiful partner, Marion. "I don't think that I'll ever be happy again, not without her. But I know I can't stay here. The memories make it all so hard." Bree looked around the room at the stacks of brown boxes that held the broken pieces of her once cheerful life. She slumped over to the side and onto the floor like a motionless blob on the carpet.

"What time are the movers coming?" Her uncle attempted a change of subject.

"Between eight and nine." Bree twirled the fibers of carpet between her fingers. "I wish they were already here. I don't know how much longer I can sit here like this." Her voice was muffled by the way her face was pressed into the floor.

"It's seven thirty. They should be there soon, kiddo. What are you doing? You sound like you have a mask on."

Bree rolled to her back and stared out the window at the blue sky full of peaceful billowing clouds. "Nothing. Why couldn't this be the crew that liked to arrive early?" Bree wasn't an impatient person. If anything, she annoyed even herself with her punctuality, but she needed to get on the road before she changed her mind again. Her depression turned back into anxiety, and she pushed herself up off the floor. "I should've just rented a truck and moved myself. It's not like I have a lot of stuff." *Not anymore.*

"Bree, relax. They'll be there soon, and it will take 'em thirty minutes to load the truck and you'll be on your way." He tried in vain to ease her stress.

Bree knew he wanted to be there with her to facilitate the move, but she needed to do it on her own. She'd made enormous strides to rebuild herself after Marion walked out on her, and she promised herself she would never again rely on anyone for anything. Even more so for things that she knew she could do on her own. While the changes she'd made were reactionary and defensive, they had allowed a glimmer of the old independent and capable Bree to shine through.

"Trust me. It's a better option than towing your car behind a giant U-Haul."

"You're probably ri—Wait. They're here!" Bree jumped up from the floor and ran to the front door when she heard the rumble of the moving van. "Okay. I'm going to watch them load my stuff, and then I'm leaving. It shouldn't take them more than thirty minutes, you said. I'm hoping to be on the turnpike by nine o'clock." Bree's calculation was optimistic.

"Okay, sweetheart. You drive careful, punkin'. Okay?" Jim always got so nervous when Bree drove long distances, especially on the major highways.

"I will. I love you, and I'll see you in fourteen hours, give or take." Before Bree said good-bye she promised him that she would be safe and at least attempt to limit her speed. She made no promises on the latter, of course.

Bree had spent four years in Boston working at the Isabella Stewart Gardner Museum. It was where she'd completed her internship in art conservation at Buffalo State and where she'd accepted her first paid staff position. At the time, she'd been ecstatic and eager to begin her career and her future. Before that, Bree always expected to return home after college. She had a plan—simple and straightforward. She would attend Buffalo State for both her bachelor's and master's degrees, complete her mandatory twelve-month internship, and then return home to a job at the infamous Biltmore Estate. Yet when the time came for Bree to follow through with the final stage of her plan, life offered her a different option—the job she'd dreamed of with a woman she loved, Marion.

Boston was a far cry from Asheville. North Carolina didn't burst at the seams with opportunities for art conservationists, yet it was where Bree's fire for art and history was ignited. Her decision to return home was a bittersweet one and a choice made more out of necessity than want. In spite of it all, she looked forward to once again feeling the sweet and unconditional love from the one person she could count on, her uncle Jim.

As a child, she often accompanied him to work and hid in the vastness and splendor that was Biltmore. He'd worked there most his life. Jim started as a stock clerk for the variety of gift and specialty shops on the property until he became the Senior Director of Engineering Services. Before Bree graduated and left for college, there was never a day she hadn't begged her uncle to take her with him to work. His boss couldn't have cared less, as Bree was "a helpful, courteous, and intelligent young lady." When she was twelve, Mr. Cordis even gifted Bree with her very own pair of white gloves for when she was "on the job."

For a curious preteen, work consisted of sitting in silence watching the conservators and technicians perform their jobs. Bree didn't mind at all. She remembered in vivid detail how she sat and studied the surgical precision of the techs as they toiled away on the objects in front of them. She admired their meticulousness, and the focus and devotion they each put into the precious items in their care. All of it was painstakingly done to ensure that future generations would someday enjoy its beauty. It was an admiration that fueled her success in the field.

When Bree had resigned her position at the Stewart Gardner, she had done so without a plan. It was a rare moment when she did anything without a strategy, but she knew that a change had to be made. After she discussed it with her uncle, she decided she would return to North Carolina in a blind attempt to pick up where her original life plan had left off. It was a decision that almost obliterated her body and soul.

Bree hadn't even left Massachusetts, and she already sensed that things weren't going to go smoothly. She experienced her first setback before she had even begun to pack. As with most museum positions, conservation openings at the Biltmore were as rare as they were competitive. It wasn't an issue she had experienced before. After all, she was a well-behaved child assistant with unlimited access to private, staff-only areas, and her own white gloves. Nevertheless, her adult self found that getting back in, even with her uncle's recommendation and influence, was more difficult than she'd anticipated.

There was no job waiting for her in North Carolina, but there was family and security. Bree had already resigned her position and sold her house, so she had no other choice but to press on. It guaranteed her momentum, because no matter how much she wanted to, there could be no turning back. When she came to terms with the idea of moving forward with her life, it made her uncertain, but it was the doing it by the seat of her pants part that petrified her.

A tragic childhood took so much from her, but it brought her Jim and more than enough money to never have to work again. And for the first time in her life, she was thankful to have a soft cushion to land on. But even with a healthy financial situation, she'd never second-guessed her desire to have a career. It was what she had always wanted since the day Jim had opened her eyes to his world. She'd had a plan from that very moment, but she strayed, and now everything in her life heaped in piles of chaos around her. She kept reminding herself that she wasn't giving up. She was just getting back onto her original path, the safe and trusted route.

She struggled to dispel the wave of nausea that swelled within her. Bree watched as the movers taped up the last of her boxes and carried them out to the truck. She would miss Boston. She would miss the friends she had made, but she could no longer tolerate the barrage of memories she experienced no matter where she went. There were very few places she could go that didn't remind her of Marion, or the life they had built and shared together. When Bree realized she avoided places she had once loved and burrowed herself in the house, she knew what she had to do.

She and the movers made one last pass through the desolate house and declared the all clear. Her stomach twisted into a coil of agony as she grabbed her bag from the counter and followed the men out the door. Bree locked up the house for the last time and gasped at the pain that threatened to squeeze her heart into dust.

Bree watched as the moving van pulled away. She got into her car but refused to look back at her house. Numb and wistful, she pulled out of the driveway and followed along behind the van that carried the shattered remnants of her life. As Bree passed familiar haunts along the route through town, she bid them a sad and silent farewell. She twisted the titanium band on her finger a few times before she removed it and dropped it down into the darkness of the center console. It was the last physical reminder of her marriage to Marion, with the exception of the yellow envelope tucked into the seat beside her. Her lawyer had drawn up the divorce papers eleven months earlier, and she had looked at them only once in all that time. They were a constant and painful memory that she couldn't yet bring herself to end. As the tears once again threatened, Bree accelerated onto the Mass Turnpike and inhaled deeply. She held the breath for several beats before she exhaled and set her sights on the road ahead. It was the road to her new beginning.

❖

Jim Whitley meandered along the path that led to the staff entrance of the sprawling, 250-room mansion known as the Biltmore Estate. Since 1895, it was America's oldest and largest privately owned home. The 179,000-square-foot house sat upon eight thousand acres of manicured and managed land with vineyards, protected forests, countless gardens, a working farm, and a five-star hotel. For over fifty years, Biltmore had prospered as a self-sufficient property with the ultimate goal of preservation for future generations. Jim had worked at Biltmore for thirty years. He started as a stock boy and ascended the ranks as a cashier, a valet, and a tour guide before working his way into property maintenance. It was in that department where he found his calling. Jim loved the responsibility and importance that came from something as simple as changing a light bulb. Preservation and conservation were of the utmost importance at Biltmore, and each job required a complete understanding of and devotion to those tenets. Jim had attended numerous workshops and classes during his employment, including a variety of accredited training courses offered by Biltmore that helped him earn a management position. He loved his job and wouldn't have traded it for the world.

Jim made his way into the mansion and passed a polished sign that hung below a velvet rope: "Restricted Area—Employees Only." Just as every good member of the Biltmore staff would, Jim reminded himself not to step on the rugs or touch any of the furnishings as he walked by. There were very few things on the property that could be touched without protective gloves. The biggest exception being one of the hundreds of brass doorknobs he reached for. He often wondered how many knobs there were on the property and why he didn't know offhand. He knew the Biltmore kept impeccable records, and if he had ever needed to know he could have found out from the one woman who ensured that each and every piece of brass in the building was kept pristine and sparkling. "I need to remember to ask her," he said to himself as he closed the door behind him.

"Ask who what?" a woman's voice questioned from across the room. She glanced up from her magnifying lamp. Before Jim answered, she'd already looked away and back down through the lens at a brilliant gilt object. Carson Harper was a conservator at the Biltmore and Jim's best friend. She analyzed an early eighteenth-century gilt wood frame. "Who?" Carson asked again as she swabbed the golden surface with what resembled an extra-large Q-Tip. When he failed to answer after several seconds, she looked up again and singsonged, "Hellooo?"

Jim enjoyed watching her work. It reminded him of when Bree had come with him and sat for hours watching the technicians work. He more than understood her lifetime fascination with it. "Huh? Oh, nothing. I was just wondering how many brass doorknobs we have and whether Julia would know," he answered.

Carson put down her tools and turned in her seat to face him. "Everybody knows that. It's six hundred and fourteen."

"What? Really? How do you kn—" Jim stopped when he saw the sarcastic look on Carson's face. "Nice. Funny."

"I know," Carson said as she turned back to her work. "Now stop bothering me. I have a lot of work to do." She shooed him away with a flick of her white-gloved hand.

"Okay." Jim turned to leave before he remembered something and turned back. "By the way, don't forget that my niece is coming home today. I'd like for us to go out to dinner when she gets settled. I think the two of you have a lot in common." Jim loved Carson, and while he hadn't always agreed with her *dating* choices, he wouldn't have minded a bit if his two favorite girls happened to hit it off. He wasn't one to play matchmaker, but he felt that each was what the other needed. If anything, he hoped that a new friendship with Carson would help heal Bree's heartbreak.

Carson had worked at the Biltmore for just under thirteen years and with Jim for the last nine. He'd watched her excel up the ranks to become one of the best and most dedicated conservationists at the estate. They'd become very close over the years. As it happened, they'd started as smoking buddies, sneaking off at any chance they could to grab a couple of puffs behind the bushes in the gardens. It wasn't long before they'd begun to spend time together outside of work. Carson didn't date, at least not in the traditional sense, and Jim hadn't been with a woman since Juliet. Over the years, they had developed a familial bond not unlike any other loving, yet, nontraditional family.

Juliet had been his one true love, and the idea of finding someone new had never been a priority for him. His priority had been to raise his beautiful niece and to make sure she would always know how much he and her parents loved her. Jim hadn't known a single thing about kids when she came to live with him. His parenting skills were rudimentary at best, and he always treated her more maturely than most would've considered reasonable for a child. Jim did the best he knew how, and in his opinion, she had grown into an exceptional woman.

Through tragedy and heartache, she had always persevered and made the best out of what life had handed her. Bree was strong, successful, and beautiful, and he was beyond proud of her. The one thing he wished was that Bree would find the one person in the world who would complement all of those wonderful qualities. She needed someone who deserved her and who would love her with as much surety and truth as he had loved his Juliet. While his heart ached for Bree and her broken heart, he had always known Marion was never that person. He loathed Marion for almost destroying the one thing on the planet he loved the most.

Carson looked back toward him with a curious look on her face. "James Whitley, are you trying to set me up with your niece?"

"What? No. No, of course not. I just thought dinner would be nice. That's all." Jim started to fidget after Carson's spot-on accusation. "I'm leaving now," he said as he hurried from the room. Her laugh faded as he continued down the hallway. He needed to admit to himself that he'd spent more than a few random moments plotting their perfect meeting. But up until then, dinner had been his best idea, though not an extraordinary one.

CHAPTER TWO

B ree approached the exit for I-81 in Pennsylvania just before two p.m. and was making decent time. Much to her uncle's chagrin, Bree preferred to call it *keeping up with traffic* rather than *speeding*. It also didn't help that her 370Z practically set its own speed. Bree zipped onto the Wilkes-Barre exit on I-81 and wondered what her uncle would say when she pulled up to the house. It wasn't often that she made a decision without consulting with him. For years, she listened to him and stuck with her loyal Lil' Red, in spite of Marion's regular expressions of disgust with the "Dumpster on wheels." But after Bree rear-ended a Highlander, the fourteen-year-old Ford with a hundred and forty-five thousand miles never bounced back. So, in what Bree declared an act of spontaneous independence, she skipped the parental approval requirement and bought the sporty coupe.

Bree belted out the words to "More Than a Woman" by the Bee Gees as she pulled her midnight blue baby into the gas station. She parked at the pump but sat in her car and sang the last verse of the song. When she got out, Bree noticed the attractive woman on the other side of the pump who stared at her with lust-filled eyes. Bree smiled in shy response and shrugged. "Good song." They both laughed at the confession.

Bree finished at the pump and went inside for a Diet Coke and a bag of pistachios. When she returned to her car, she noticed that the woman had crossed over to her side to inspect Bree's Nissan. "Gorgeous, isn't she?" Bree asked.

"Yes. And the car isn't bad either," the tall, slender brunette said.

Bree blushed at the overused cliché and hated that she'd fallen for it. Marion always used the same confident cockiness to get into or out of just about everything. "Thanks," Bree snapped as she reached for the door.

"Just out for a drive or is there someplace you have to be right away?" the woman asked.

Just like Marion, this woman didn't pick up on disinterest, blatant or subtle. "I'm on my way home." The woman raised an inquisitive eyebrow. "No, I mean home, as in North Carolina. Just stopping for gas and a Diet Coke." Bree held up the bottle as proof.

"Oh, that's unfortunate, for both of us. Allow me," the woman said as she slid off to the side, out of Bree's way. She made a sweeping gesture and opened Bree's car door. "Drive safely."

She forced a kind "thank you" and got into the car. "I got it." Bree grabbed the door handle with a stiff arm and stopped the woman as she attempted to close it for her. Bree did little to mask what had now become a mix of disgust and irritation. It was then that Bree's apathy registered with the other woman. She threw her hands up and backed away with exaggerated indignation. Bree rolled her eyes but said nothing as she pulled the handle and closed the door. She sat behind the wheel and watched as the woman's car pulled out of the station. She slammed her head back into the headrest. "When did I become such an asshole?"

It may have been a rhetorical question, but it had an actual answer. She hoped her return home would resurrect the old Bree, although she had serious doubts that she still existed. Irritated at herself, Bree shifted into first gear and spun her tires on the way out of the parking lot.

The sudden rush of speed and adrenaline made her grin. For an instant, Bree felt free and unburdened even if her actions were careless and unnecessary. It reminded her of how nervous Jim had been when he'd taught her how to drive. It was recalling his sadness and trepidation that made her put a damper on her burst of recklessness. It was what kept her safe, as well as revived the painful memories of everything she'd lost and found.

Bree was not the best driver even though she tried to be for both her sake and Jim's. She knew all too well why Uncle Jim was so nervous when she drove anywhere. Bree had just turned eight years old when her parents and Jim's wife were killed in a horrific wreck on their way home from dinner. Jim's survival of the accident that took his only brother, sister-in-law, and his beloved Juliet was nothing less than a miracle. There weren't many, including Bree's grandparents, who held out hope that if Jim managed to recover that he would make it through the grief. They said it wasn't until Jim learned he had become Bree's legal guardian that he had begun to improve.

While her uncle never talked about the accident, Bree once found a box that contained old photographs and newspaper articles. Images of the scene, and what remained of the vehicles involved, were forever branded in her mind. Bree was thankful every day of her life that she still had Jim in it. She thought about her mother and father often, but when someone mentioned a parent, it was always her uncle's face that came to mind first.

Once, when Bree was a teenager, they had discussed her parents and what, if anything, she remembered of them. It was then that she had learned about her substantial inheritance. Yet no money in the world could have brought them back or made up for all she had lost. She remembered the sadness in his eyes when she told him that what she would miss the most were the moments she would never have. As the years passed, her memories faded and what remained centered around the funeral and the short time she'd spent at her grandparents' house before Jim had taken her home. He was all she had left then and he was all she had left now.

Bree was thankful when the chime of her low-fuel warning brought her out of the dark memories. She scanned the interstate signs for an upcoming exit where she would stop for gas. Roanoke, Virginia. As she pulled off the highway, she knew that the next time she would need gas, she would be there. *Home.*

❖

As usual, Carson waited for Jim in the hallway before their joint department staff meeting. He always attended every meeting that involved the main house, even if it wasn't required. One of the things that made Jim so successful was his ability to keep everyone included and informed. To Carson, he was a mentor as well as a friend and father figure.

In the beginning of their friendship, most people didn't understand what she could have had in common with a man thirty years her senior. There was no doubt that everyone assumed such a relationship involved sex or money, or both. It had not. It didn't surprise her when she learned that a handful of the nosey know-it-alls believed she and Jim were engaged in what they deemed an "inappropriate relationship." She wasn't sure what constituted inappropriate, but in the end, it had been a brief rumor. It was quashed by a racier truth once

Carson had been caught kissing Kristina, the gorgeous, female floral designer. In an instant, the close connection she had with Jim was the least inappropriate thing about any of Carson's relationships. Over the years, Carson's sexuality was no longer the subject of relentless hen talk, and she became just another part of the Biltmore family. As with many families, it was with love that they protected her with ferocity and harassed her with relentlessness. She loved every minute of it.

Carson was confident, and she knew that confidence was more than half of what drew women to her. There was no doubt her smile didn't hurt. For a while, it wasn't often that Carson turned a woman down. Gay, straight, bi, or married—it never mattered to her. She couldn't deny that she had a fair number of casual affairs with most of the young ladies that crossed her path. As she'd gotten older, Carson still attracted plenty of random glances and advances, but she had become more discerning about when and where she acted upon her desires. At least she liked to think so. She told herself it was because of work and that she needed to be focused on her career and future. But it may have been more about her aversion to long-term commitment, because the older she got, the more difficult it had become to avoid.

Long-term relationships did not hold the same comfortable appeal to her as they did for every other woman she knew. She had never met one who she could honestly imagine herself sharing every part of her life with. The idea of side-by-side toothbrushes and Sunday trips to the grocery store was just a smidge less horrifying than having to tell someone every move three weeks in advance. It wasn't impossible, just improbable.

Carson glanced at her watch just as the door opened, and Jim sauntered toward her.

"Don't you know it's rude to keep a lady waiting?" Carson tapped the face of her watch.

"A lady? Where?" Jim leaned and looked around Carson.

Carson punched him in the arm. "Asshole." They both laughed on their way down the hall to the meeting that had already begun.

Jim rubbed his wounded arm as they slipped into the room and into two available seats near the back. A couple of women on the opposite side of the room demanded Carson's attention. The young, attractive blondes blushed and waved their fingers at her. Becky and Lisa were interns in the curatorial department, and they were relentless in their pursuit of Carson's free time. There had been a time when she would've fallen all over herself to have two gorgeous women share her bed, or wherever else they might have ended up.

"Damn. What the hell is wrong with me?" Carson whispered to Jim.

"What are you talking about?"

"I've got to be an idiot to keep turning those girls down. Together, at least." She raised her eyebrows.

Jim shook his head. "Maybe you're growing up. Plus, don't you think Becky is enough for any one person?"

Carson scoffed. "Maybe I'm getting old. Sex isn't worth all the drama that comes along with it." She turned her attention back to the chief curator, who now spoke about the latest project approvals and staff openings.

Carson had been promoted to conservator three years earlier. She had worked her way up from where she started as an intern in Textiles. The Biltmore was her first real job out of college. She had opted for the position even after she already completed a one-year internship in Italy as required for her degree from Columbia. In the beginning, Carson thought her time at the Biltmore would be short. Her plan had been to gain experience and knowledge and then move on. That had been thirteen years earlier, and she had no intention of leaving. Of course, she was sure to always leave open the option in case something better came along. It was the freedom to choose that she liked to maintain.

Carson's vision of the future was simple and uncomplicated. She always expected herself to become a chief curator somewhere, maybe at the Biltmore, maybe someplace on the other side of the country, or even on the other side of the world. She would never dismiss the possibility of one day having a beautiful house, a wife, and maybe even a child or two, but for now and the foreseeable future, she was more than content with her life as it was.

Carson's thoughts were disrupted by an elbow in her side and someone saying her name. She glared over at Jim. "What the fu—" She stopped short when he cleared his throat and motioned his eyes toward the woman who stood at the front of the room. The chief curator's eyes were one pair of many that stared in her direction. Her boss, Beth Daniels, looked at her with one sharp raised eyebrow.

"Well, it appears Carson isn't interested. So, is there anyone else interested in being the lead on the third-floor project?" Beth scanned the room filled with smiling faces. Some of them looked at Beth while everyone else looked at Carson.

Carson's face reddened. "I'm so sorry, Beth, uh, Mrs. Daniels. I was thinking…I was distracted…I mean…" Carson gave up her search for an excuse. She sank down into her chair and slapped a hand over her face. Carson was far from a slacker. She had always taken her job more seriously than most because she loved what she did. Even Carson was surprised that she didn't have a legitimate reason for why she had failed to pay the least bit of attention in the meeting.

When Carson heard her boss laugh, followed by the chuckles of her coworkers, she looked up. The red glow returned to her cheeks. "Carson, will you come up here, please?" Beth motioned for Carson to join her at the front of the room.

The laughter quieted once she reached the front of the room. Beth wrapped her arm around Carson's shoulders. She pulled her in close and whispered in her ear, "I really caught you off guard that time. I cannot believe you weren't paying attention at all." Beth snickered.

Carson had a jokester side to her, and Beth had always been the easiest of all her victims. There was a time when Carson had quite a crush on Beth. Her practical jokes had begun as immature attempts to flirt with the older, more mature, and much straighter, Beth Daniels. "Yeah, I'll give you that one."

Beth made the official announcement of Carson's appointment as the lead conservator for the third floor restoration project, known as the Maid Suites. After a round of congratulatory applause, Carson thanked everyone and returned to her seat.

Jim gave her a nudge and wrapped his arm around her shoulder for a squeeze. "Now let that be a lesson in why you should always pay attention at meetings."

Carson pushed him off with a playful shove and crossed her arms. "A real friend would have warned me," she said before she stuck her tongue out at him.

"Very mature, Ms. Harper. I take back my comment about you growing up," Jim said as he winked.

CHAPTER THREE

Bree spent most of the weekend at home slowly unpacking her things. Late on Sunday night, several of the boxes marked "Do Not Open/Storage" remained stacked and unopened near the garage door. She knew what they contained, and the markings were a warning to her head and her heart to avoid their contents. Most of the boxes had been packed up long before Bree had decided to move, and even then the project had taken her a year to muster the strength to complete.

When Marion left, she'd taken everything with her. But that had been Bree's idea, or at least she thought it had been. She couldn't remember much of the day Marion had returned with the moving van and carried out the pieces of the life they had built together. All she'd left were tokens and trinkets that counted the lost years and memories. They remained scattered around the house for almost a year before Bree could pack them away out of sight. The thing that prevented her from throwing them out then was the same thing that put them on the truck and hauled them with her to North Carolina. Hope.

Bree didn't have much in the way of furniture or household goods, so she was glad that the house was already furnished. It was a detached two-story, three-bedroom, two-bath home that sat just up a small hill from the main house where her uncle lived. She and Jim had purchased the property the summer before she left for college. It was the one real extravagance that they'd ever used Bree's inheritance for. She'd never lived in the house, and she had preferred to stay in the main house with him when she visited, which unfortunately, wasn't as much as she'd have liked. Bree had always hoped that one day she and Marion would move to North Carolina to start a family in the house. But her love for North Carolina was far greater than Marion's, so there was always a different reason or excuse as to why they "couldn't make it for a visit this year." After a few years, Jim had simply stopped asking when he'd see her again. As had become the norm, the thoughts of what should've been brought on the waves of sickness. When Bree could no longer sit around in the quiet and think about the what-ifs, she forced herself off the couch and shuffled down the hall to bed.

Bree woke in a cheerful mood early on Monday morning and headed over to the main house. She wanted to tag along with Jim to work, and her plan was to make breakfast as a means to bribe him into letting her. If she sat alone in her house for another minute, she would've gone out of her mind. Bree knew the best way to her uncle's heart was with cheesy grits and greasy bacon. Although she couldn't stand grits, Jim always seemed to love the way she made them. In fact, she despised a lot of foods that her uncle enjoyed. She blamed it on the texture and her uncontrollable need to chew everything to mush before she was able to swallow it. Bree was not a chef, but she found her way around the kitchen well enough. At least well enough to keep herself from starving to death. Of course that was if she had any food to cook, because if there was one thing she hated worse than eating mushrooms and sweet potatoes, it was shopping for them. She was thankful for the big-box retailers that sold household goods and groceries along with clothes and shoes.

As Bree leaned into the refrigerator for breakfast ingredients, she chuckled at the memories of when her uncle bribed her with toys or charms in exchange for good behavior. It was more of a tradition and less of a disciplinary tactic since Bree never misbehaved.

Bree removed a pot from the stove and stirred the "corn sludge" as she mumbled to herself. "Yuck. You could lay bricks with this crap."

Out of the quiet, a man's voice boomed behind her. "Still not fond of grits, huh?"

Bree jerked back and flung a spoonful of grits into the air. "Dammit! You scared the shit out of me."

"Looks like I scared the *grits* out of you," he said as they both stared at the thick glob of goo that oozed down the surface of the oak cabinet. Bree eyed Jim before they erupted with laughter.

"Here." With a gentle grin, Bree shoved the bowl in his direction and sprinkled cheese onto the top.

"Thanks, Breezy." He leaned in to kiss her on the cheek and took the bowl at the same time. "So, to what do I owe this beautiful surprise?" Jim raised an eyebrow at her as he sat in a chair at the table.

Bree wiped the thick sticky mess off the cabinet and then put the bacon on a plate. She balanced it carefully on top of one of the coffee cups she carried to the table. "Oh, nothing. Just thought I'd make breakfast." He tilted his head in disbelief. "Okay, fine. I was trying to bribe you into taking me to work with you today." She smiled at him and batted her eyelashes just like she had done when she was younger. It always worked like a charm, and this time was no exception.

"Like I could ever say no to my punkin' when she looks at me like that." He gave her a gentle pinch on her cheek before giving it a little smack. "Brat."

"Yay!" Bree jumped up from her seat and spun around. "Okay. You eat, and I'm going to go get dressed. I can't wait to see the house and Julie. Is Julie still there? How about Ms. Carmichael? Does she still pretend to be a cranky old lady? Oh. And Barbara. Yay! I'll be back." Bree didn't give her uncle a second to respond as she spun like a whirlwind through the kitchen and out the door.

Bree showered, dressed, and was back in the kitchen in record time. She finished her coffee and tapped her nail on the side of the mug while she waited impatiently for her uncle. She was just as excited to go with him as an adult as she had been as a child. Bree paced around the kitchen until Jim came down. She set her mug into the sink, gave one last skip, and shouted "Yay!" before they headed out the door.

❖

Bree and Jim lived about twenty minutes from the Biltmore gates. The house and staff parking lot was another two and a half miles in via service roads. The visitors and guests used the three-mile-long Approach Road that followed the original driveway designed by Frederick Law Olmstead in 1895. It was a beautiful drive that very few people took the time to enjoy on their way up to the mansion. While the service roads lacked the formal designs and landscaping of Approach Road, Bree still enjoyed the beautiful forest around them. It was a small portion of the estimated twenty thousand acres of managed forest. And it was still just a small segment of the more than one hundred thousand original acres that George Vanderbilt owned when the Biltmore Forest School was established in 1898. The remainder of the forest was sold to the government in 1914 and became part of the Pisgah National Forest.

As they approached the staff parking area, Bree's heart

raced. She was almost unable to keep herself from jumping from the vehicle and running into the building. She couldn't wait to see everyone and everything that she'd missed so much over the many years she'd been away. Until that moment she hadn't realized just how much that was. Bree had been home for just a few days and already she felt younger and happier than she had in years.

Bree vibrated with excitement, and Jim would have had to be dead not to notice. He had slowed down through the parking lot and exaggerated his search for a perfect spot. She looked over at him every few moments as she gripped the door handle and anxiously tapped her foot. When she'd had enough, Bree grumbled and looked over at him. He exploded with laughter when her comprehension of his antics registered. "Are you serious?" Bree yelled and slapped him in the arm. She unlatched her seat belt in haste and demanded that he "park the damn truck already." He continued to laugh even after he had pulled into a spot, turned off the truck, and watched as she leapt from the vehicle.

Bree grabbed his arm and pulled him close in a side hug. She refrained, albeit just, from slinging herself onto his back for a piggyback ride like she had always done as a child. To quell her excitement, she opted to link his arm with hers instead.

❖

Carson woke in a haze and rolled onto her back. The movement caused her head to swim. She felt as if she were on a boat as it sloshed relentlessly in a windy harbor. She slapped her arms out to her sides and hoped that a firm grip on the mattress would reduce the ebb and flow of her bed. Carson cursed herself for giving in to the charms of the smooth-talking "Señor Patron" the night before. She looked around the room. Something wasn't right. Carson's first thought was that she had fallen asleep with her bedroom lights on again. It didn't take her long to realize that the light was natural and it flooded in through the open curtains. She thrashed her arm up and down on the bed and tried to locate her phone. The quick movements encouraged the dull knock that had already begun in her head.

She slowed her search to soft pats out of fear that she would rile her stomach next. Carson located the elusive device and begged the powers that be for it to be Saturday. She knew very well that it wasn't Saturday, but she still hoped like hell it was before she looked at the screen. *Monday. 10:03 a.m.* "Son of a bitch!" Carson said as she kicked the covers off and jolted upright. She realized her mistake and sprinted toward the bathroom.

Carson still felt like the undead even after she had showered and dressed. She popped a cup into her coffee maker and stared with a lifeless expression as it steamed and hissed. Carson hoped that the double mug of coffee and four pain relievers would be enough to at least get her through the drive into work. After that, it was up to the hangover gods. "You never learn," she admonished herself. She sat at the table with her cup and dialed work. Even though Beth didn't care, she needed to let her boss know she would be late. It wasn't until Carson hung up that she noticed the seven missed text messages. Instinct told her that no less than half of them were from Becky, and one click into her message folder confirmed it. Carson chose to read the two texts from Jim, as she'd not had enough caffeine to deal with the others.

She messaged Jim back quickly. *No. I'm not dead. At least I don't think so. See you in a bit.-C*

His response was almost immediate and he let her know

that Becky had already managed to tell everyone about the night they'd spent together.

Like most of her couplings, it was a relationship built on physical attraction alone, and Carson had been just fine with that. Becky was adventurous and uninhibited, and that made things fast and hot—just how Carson liked it. Everything was going good until Becky implied that she had begun to develop feelings for Carson. While Carson was fond of Becky as a person, there were more than a handful of reasons why a long-term relationship with Becky was not an option, even beyond Carson's own misgivings.

After Becky's "I have feelings" declaration, Carson was honest when she explained things to her. She just didn't feel the same way, and she didn't think she ever would. To her surprise, Becky had taken the information rather well and agreed without hesitation to a simple friends with benefits arrangement. The idea had been Becky's, and Carson's acceptance of the proposal was selfish. After all, what sort of dolt would turn down the potential for hot, commitment-free sex? In spite of its availability, Carson tried not to redeem the benefits of the agreement very often. The exception being when she and her conscience were under the influence of far too many shots of tequila—like the night before.

Carson didn't respond to Becky's messages. She decided it was time to nip the whole thing in the bud. It was clear that Becky had not understood the meaning of discretion as it related to their casual relationship. It was one Carson never should've started in the first place, and she knew it was the right thing to do. She also knew that it needed to be done before it interfered any further with her career and her coworkers. She had a fifteen-minute drive accompanied by a screaming headache to think of a diplomatic and non-confrontational way to pull it off, even if she had to lie a little.

CHAPTER FOUR

B ree meandered through the lobby. She spent the first three hours hugging what seemed like every person in the building. After she finished visiting, Bree left her uncle to his work and set off to spend the remainder of the day playing tourist. She started out in the grand foyer. She closed her eyes and listened to the hustle of the families and the echoes of voices that filled the vaulted space. Bree tried to recall the last time that she had taken the actual self-guided tour but couldn't. She came to the immediate conclusion that she had never walked through the estate and viewed the art and architecture as a mere layperson. She had always just followed her uncle or others around and viewed the rooms and their contents from an insider's perspective. The idea of seeing things with fresh eyes excited her.

From the onset of her tour, Bree noticed the speed of the impatient visitors. Children and families zipped along through the rooms as if on a supersonic time schedule. Bree wasn't surprised. She'd seen it in every museum she had ever been to, including the Gardner. After all, it was the technological age. She imagined that just getting their kids to look up from their games was hard enough when you didn't make walking and learning about "old stuff" the singular alternative. Bree made a quick mental note about video games for when and if she ever had children.

Bree strolled through the entrance hall and followed it around to the Winter Garden. It was an interior tropical oasis illuminated by an ornate ceiling of wood and glass. At its center stood the sculpture of *Boy Stealing Geese* by Karl Bitter. Like most rooms in the chateau, the Winter Garden's décor was changed based on holidays or specially recognized days, such as the Vanderbilts' wedding anniversary.

Bree ambled along behind a small group of older women that she had unassumingly adopted as her own personal tour group. They moved through the building at a comfortable pace and expressed an honorable interest in their surroundings. Bree appreciated that. She overheard one of the women ask a question that no one could answer, so Bree offered one. From that point, she became the group's unofficial guide to Biltmore.

Bree enjoyed her unplanned tour guide duties. The Biltmore had a team of exceptional docents who led various paid tours throughout the property. Conducting an unsanctioned tour would have been frowned upon by house staff had she not been Mr. James Whitley's daughter. She stood on the second step of the Grand Staircase while her small, private group hovered around her and hung on every word as Bree described the design and construction of the marble steps. Bree paused her lecture in mid-sentence when something across the room caught her attention. Her eyes locked onto a figure that sprinted through the hall toward her and her group. The person darted toward them with determined intent. The moment their eyes met, a searing rush of electricity surged through her. It was in that same moment that Bree realized it was a woman. The woman was solid, tall, and breathtaking and her jet-black hair was short and wild. Her blue button-down shirt was tucked into a smooth-fitting pair of dark blue jeans. Her movement was effortless as she leapt onto the second step without a break in stride. The sudden movement startled Bree, and she jumped back to avoid a collision but dared not break eye contact.

She had never seen eyes so blue in all her life. Bree had never been so hypnotized by anything, and time ceased. The woman offered a captivating smile, and Bree's breath caught in her chest. Her legs wobbled beneath her as she was bombarded by the crisp, intoxicating scent of cologne. Bree's body burned as she watched the woman bound up the stairs. When she disappeared around the curve of the steps, Bree closed her eyes. She took another deep breath and allowed the moment to sear into her mind.

Through what felt like cotton in her ears, someone spoke her name. She opened her eyes and noticed the six intrigued women who stared back at her. "I'm sorry about that, ladies. I was a little startled, but I'm fine now." Bree tried like hell to push the image of the woman from her mind.

"Wow. She was quite attractive wasn't she?" Bree heard one of the ladies say to the others.

"Yes. If I was thirty years younger, I'd have run up those steps after her." The announcement was acknowledged by a sharp smack in the arm from a map held by the woman next to her.

Bree was surprised she hadn't noticed it earlier. It was clear to her now that her adopted tour family was more *family* than she had realized at the onset. As the women continued to stare at her, Bree's feelings of exhilaration and attraction were overpowered by the feelings of guilt and shame. She scolded herself for the raw and uncontrolled reaction to another woman. Yet beyond that, Bree felt in that moment as if every void within her had been filled. She cursed Marion for being the very reason for the vast emptiness inside her. She had been so strong until then and she refused to let herself break.

She pushed back the darkness of pain that spread through her heart, and with the confidence that she didn't possess, she led her new friends up the stairs.

A small part of Bree had hoped the woman with raven hair waited for her at the top of the steps. Just when she thought her heart rate had returned to normal, it increased again. With each rise, her anticipation grew. *What if she is there? Waiting? What would I possibly say to her?* When they reached the second floor, the ladies expressed their obvious displeasure that the woman was nowhere in sight. Bree remained silent, torn between disappointment and relief.

The women wove through the second-floor rooms, which included the bedroom suites of George and Edith Vanderbilt. Edith's room was one of Bree's favorites in the house. She had always been impressed by the vast amount of gold that the room contained. It made Bree feel as if she were able to swim in the countless yards of gold silk that poured like gilt waterfalls around the room. Bree was mesmerized by the extravagance of it. There were few things in her life that affected her with the same intensity. The Hall of Mirrors at Versailles, the ceiling of the Sistine Chapel in Rome, a night launch of the Space Shuttle *Discovery*, and now, the brilliant eyes of the mysterious woman that captivated her mind.

Bree and her ladies ambled through the other rooms while they joked about the lavatories and made racy comments about the servants' quarters. She enjoyed overloading them with a variety of fun facts and rumors that helped keep her mind off her recent encounter. Her new friends were fun, entertaining, and curious, and Bree was glad that fate had brought them together.

Of the six women, Gwen and Suzanne were her favorites. Gwen was sarcastic and the clear leader of the group. Suzanne was Gwen's partner of thirty years and was a perfect introverted complement to her extroverted spouse. Their love was undeniable and their connection was obvious to anyone who looked at them. The ease with which they loved each other was the one thing Bree thought she might not have had with Marion. She had loved her with all her heart. But was it ever so effortless? Bree tried to remember through the fog of time, and her heart clenched at the thought of forgetting. She was being ridiculous. Of course it had been that same love. Their arrival at the recently unveiled Louis VX Suites brought Bree out of a potential downward spiral.

Bree was excited to have the opportunity to see the completed project. She was in awe from the moment she laid eyes on the striking fabric and wallpaper reproductions. Her uncle had told her that they'd found a company in France that reproduced the exquisite fabric by hand, a process which had taken more than two years to complete. Bree slipped on her headphones and pressed play on her audio device. She listened as the narrator discussed the fine details of the restoration. She and the ladies dispersed and drifted in silence as they surveyed the new rooms on their own.

In an instant, the women were bombarded by an enormous group of people that had materialized around them. The group was loud and erratic as they swarmed into the small room. Bree was forced to step forward to avoid being trampled by the throng of rude people that were oblivious of her presence. She felt a sharp object, possibly an elbow, jam into her back, and she lunged forward. Bree extended her arms and placed her hands on the chair in front of her for stability. Although caught off guard by the jolt, she was thrilled by the feel of the fabric under hers fingers, so soft and plush. She ripped her hands from the furniture as if she'd been burned. She couldn't believe what she had done. In the confusion of impolite and pushy people, she had lost all common sense as well as the basics of her education.

Even though it was a complete accident, she admonished herself. "Without gloves." As any guilty person would do, Bree looked around to see if there had been witnesses. A small child looked up at her with wide eyes and an open mouth. "Oops." Bree shrugged and forced a smile at the little girl. Bree decided that she would slink away in shame in an attempt to avoid being confronted by security in front of a room full of people.

❖

Carson was late for work, so she didn't think that taking a few extra minutes to talk to Becky would make much of a difference. While the thought of having a conversation with Becky while she suffered from a miserable hangover didn't sit well with her, she couldn't put it off. Becky had been working with the Textiles team on the Louis rooms, so Carson beelined across the foyer toward the staircase. It was both the quickest and the easiest way to get there. She sprinted across the length of the room toward a group of ladies that mingled at the bottom of the steps. All of the women save one stepped back and made way for her. Without breaking stride, Carson leapt onto the second step. It was then that this woman attempted to move in order to avoid an impact. The startled woman's eyes were wide, and Carson was captured by them.

The woman was gorgeous and stood out from everyone around her in both age and beauty. She was short and beautiful. Her warm, sun-soaked blond hair and deep brown eyes consumed Carson's consciousness. Her hair was tied back in a haphazard coif with wild and unruly curls. Carson gave the woman her most delightful smile. She fought back the sudden desire she had to stop dead in her tracks and speak to her. She was on a mission, but she didn't need to look back to know that the woman's eyes were still on her. She felt the gaze as she continued up the stairs. The heat burned through her body even after she reached the second floor landing. Carson hoped the conversation with Becky would be a quick one so she might find a way to cross paths with the alluring stranger elsewhere in the building.

Carson found Becky right where she'd expected to. For Carson, the key to cutting off girls like her was to keep things simple and focus on the positives. It was a proven tactic perfected by experience. Except with Becky, Carson was lured into continued contact with the promise of good sex. This time, she had to break it off completely—just friends and no sex, period. Carson motioned to get Becky's attention and waved her over.

"Hey, baby. How are you feeling?" Becky smiled and reached out to stroke Carson's arm.

Carson slid Becky's hand off her arm and down to Becky's side. "I'm all right. A little hungover, of course, but otherwise I'm fine."

"I was worried about you this morning when you didn't text me back, baby."

"Becky, we need to talk. And please stop calling me baby," Carson whispered as she led Becky back into the corner of the room.

Becky's eyes lit up with anticipation for an intimate moment in the corner with Carson. She pushed her body in closer, and Carson backed away. When Becky moved in again, Carson's back pressed against the wall. She placed her hands on Becky's shoulders to put some distance between them. She swung around with the openness now behind her. Becky looked at Carson with confusion. "What's wrong with you, Carson?"

"Nothing. We just need to talk about last night."

"It was nice, wasn't it?"

"Yes. No. I mean look. We can't do this anymore. We talked about this, and it's not fair to keep holding you back when you have so much ahead of you," Carson explained. "You have so much talent. I think you should focus on your internship and moving on from here. You and me, it was fun, but I can't give you what you want and it's selfish of me to lead you on."

"Lead me on? I'm a big girl, you know. I can make my own decisions."

"That's not what I meant. I mean—" Carson started again.

"Oh. So I'm good enough to fuck, but not good enough for a relationship?"

"That's not what I said. At all." Carson backtracked. "Becky, please don't be like that. We both agreed that our relationship would stay physical. And I just think it's time for you to start focusing more on your future and less on me, on sex. That's all."

"Carson, we could work on it, you know. You could start to like me for more than sex. But you won't. What are you afraid of?"

"I'm not afraid of anything, Becky. I just can't give you what you want. I know this is for the best."

Becky crossed her arms. "Whatever. You don't even know what I want."

Carson knew what Becky wanted. She wanted a long-term relationship. She wanted Carson to fall in love with her and have babies, but it just wasn't going to happen. Becky had years of life to live before she needed to think about settling down. Carson knew who she was and was living the life she had worked for. Becky was just starting out, and Carson didn't want to relive those parts of her life again. The room started to fill with people, and Carson knew she needed to end the conversation. "I'm sorry, Becky. I am. We can talk more later if you want. I've got to get downstairs."

"Yeah, fine. Whatever. I need to go find Mr. Whitley anyway," Becky said as she left the room.

Carson saw that Becky's eyes glossed, yet she didn't see the emotion that should have accompanied the tears. She hadn't expected to get away without making Becky cry, so she was a little surprised that in addition to relief she also felt selfish and disappointed. "That was easy."

Carson smoothed down her shirt and stepped out into the crowd. She spotted the woman from the staircase and stepped back again. She tried as best she could to blend into the wall behind her. Carson watched as the woman looked around frantically as the herd of people pushed their way in toward her. Carson also watched in disbelief as the woman reached out and clenched onto the refurbished, 110-year-old damask chair on the other side of the rope barrier.

Carson was disgusted by the woman's apparent lack of respect for Biltmore property and for the rules of the estate. Either the woman was unable to read the hundreds of posted signs that stated "Do not touch" or she was just another entitled jerk who lacked any respect for history. She had seen it a hundred times during her internship in Italy, and she despised the audacity of such people.

Carson waited for a guard to appear. They would either give the woman a warning or escort her from the premises. The reprimand would depend on if this was her first offense or not. The woman possessed a confidence that was obvious by how she carried herself. It was intriguing and sexy, and seduced Carson in an unfamiliar way. She continued to observe the woman as she proceeded into the next room. *Wait. Where are the guards?* Carson scanned the area for security that she would have expected already. Lacking any presence of guard personnel, Carson took on the responsibility and followed the woman, her head still hammering away. It wasn't a wholly undesirable decision.

CHAPTER FIVE

Carson weaved with purpose through the crowd toward the blonde who stood in the middle of a small group of women. One of them spotted Carson as she approached and attempted to hide the look of surprise on her face. Carson watched the woman nudge the person beside her and whisper something. Whatever it was caused the others to snap their heads in her direction, including the one she was after. Carson's forward movement stopped when her eyes met the dark brown ones that stared back at her. The young woman's eyes were wide with surprise. Carson was intrigued as she watched the emotions battling on the woman's beautiful face.

She had smooth, porcelain skin with flushed cheeks and natural pink lips. The charged and unflinching gaze melted Carson from the inside out. She was overwhelmed with the swirl of energy that stirred in the space between them. Carson had never before experienced such a magnetic and brain-scrambling pull to be closer to another person. She stopped in her tracks, having all but forgotten why she pursued the woman in the first place.

When a security guard tapped the woman on the shoulder, she was reminded of why she had pursued her. Carson felt as though all the air rushed from the room the moment she looked away. The fire that burned inside her was snuffed out and left her with an unusual and peculiar chill. Carson could not shake the desire to be closer, to at least hear her voice. As the woman and her group acknowledged the guard, Carson approached them. She would use the excuse that she acted on behalf of the estate if anyone questioned her presence.

Carson's previous anger had almost dissipated, having been overshadowed by far more intense feelings. However, the woman had activated the alarm, and regardless of her exceptional beauty, she needed to be confronted about her negligence. As Carson's heart rate increased so did the pounding in her head.

"Hello, ma'am. It appears that you touched a piece of furniture in the other room. And—"

"No. I didn't. See, it was—" The woman took an unexpected and defensive stance and was interrupted by the guard.

Carson was surprised at the woman's attempt to deny any wrongdoing. Even without the alarms and video system, Carson had witnessed it. *Don't deny it.* She squeezed the bridge of her nose as her head increased its pounding cadence. *Just admit it and move on.*

"Ma'am, the alarm," he said as he pointed to the inconspicuous light that strobed in the corner of the room. It was accompanied by the subtle and distant ring of a bell.

"But I didn't. I mean it was an—" the woman stuttered. Carson found it hard to believe that she still attempted to deny it.

"Yes, ma'am, you did. I was there," Carson stated matter-of-factly as a means to resolve the situation.

The woman spun around and glared at Carson. Her expression morphed through surprise and embarrassment to anger. *She's mad? This woman is going to get defensive about something we have proof she did? She's even gorgeous when she's mad.*

"No. I mean, yes. I did, but—" The woman's eyes burned with a heat that could have been interpreted as either passion or fury.

"So you did or you didn't?" Carson was encouraged by the woman's struggle to defend herself and the fire in her stare.

"If you would stop interrupting me, I would explain to you." The woman placed her hands on her hips.

Carson almost smiled at her defiance. It was unbelievably sexy. "Explain what? That you can't read? That you didn't think the signs and notices applied to you?" Carson had no idea why she rattled the woman's cage, but she enjoyed it with devilish enthusiasm.

"Oh, my God. Are you serious? Who are you and what gives you the right to speak to me like this? I touched the damn chair. I'm sorry and I feel horrible about it. It was an accident."

"We work very hard here to preserve and protect these treasures for the future, and people like you—" Carson was silenced by the guard's firm hand on her shoulder. By the look on his face, he was taken aback by her unordinary sternness.

"Ms. Harper, I can handle this, ma'am. It's okay. I'm certain she understands the impact of her actions and will not make the mistake again. Is that correct, ma'am?" The guard looked back and forth between them.

"People like me?" she asked Carson. "Oh, I understand. Ms. Harper, was it? And believe me when I say that there will be two of us not making the same mistake twice."

Carson heard the threat and wrestled to hold back a smile. "Well, I can hope you won't, but I wouldn't place bets on it." Carson winked at the woman, thanked the guard, and sauntered out of the room before she even had a chance to retort.

As Carson headed down to her office, she reprimanded herself for the way she had acted. Her head hammered with every step she took down the stairs. She shouldn't have gotten involved. She should've waited for the guards. It was their job, not hers, but something inside Carson was drawn to the woman. It was almost primal, and as the woman grew more agitated, Carson grew more ravenous.

She pushed the door open, and it stopped with a thud. Carson heard someone grunt in pain followed by a yell. "Seriously?" Carson nudged the door open and peeked inside. Jim backed away as he grasped his hand and grimaced.

"Damn, girl. Where's the fire?" he asked while he rubbed his wounded fingers.

"Right here," she said as she clutched her chest where her heart pounded. "Do you ever have those days where you don't think you should get out of bed?"

"Sometimes. Why?"

"Because I thought that was the kind of day it was going to be. Turns out, it's not as bad as I thought."

"Well, that's great, kiddo. Mine was good before someone went and broke my damn fingers." He exaggerated a frown. "Oh, Bree is here, and I want you to meet her when you get a second. She's upstairs pretending to be a tourist."

Carson liked the way Jim's face lit up when he spoke about his niece, and it made her smile. "Great. I look forward to it. Tell her to watch out for a terribly gorgeous rule-breaking menace I just left up there."

"Um, okay then. I'll let her know."

After Jim left, Carson sat at her worktable and pulled herself close to the ceramic sculpture she needed to finish cleaning. It was a tedious job, but she loved it and it cleared her head of anything and everything around her. Everything except for the way the woman had looked at her. The raw looks of desire, fear, and anger were scorched into Carson's body and mind.

❖

As soon as he left Carson's office, Jim's phone rang. "Hey, Breezy, where are you?" Jim hadn't expected the frustration he heard in her voice. "Whoa, kiddo. Slow down. What happened? I'll be right there." Jim headed off to find Bree and figure out what in the world had her so enraged.

He found Bree in the entranceway. She paced back and forth in a group of older ladies who stood around while they cooed and murmured at her. He had no idea who the women were or why they consoled her. "Hey," he said while he looked around at the ladies who scrutinized his presence.

Bree looked at him. She was on the verge of tears, and that meant one of two things. She was either devastated or furious. By the tone of her voice on the phone, he went with the latter. "I have never been so disrespected in all my life. I am not a child. I know very well what I did. I didn't try to deny it or make excuses. Who does she think she is?" Bree took a shallow breath.

"Calm down. What are you talking about, sweetheart?" He looked around at the women again. It was obvious that they knew something that he didn't. He raised his eyebrows in question, but they offered nothing. He turned back to Bree. "Bree, look at me. What happened?"

"That woman. I touched a chair. It was an accident. There were so many people, I was just trying to get out of their way. But she saw me. She said she saw me, and she attacked me."

"Attacked? Someone attacked you? Sit down, here." Jim led her to a bench to sit down. "Relax for a minute." Bree shook with anger. He looked at one of the women who stood behind him. "I'm her uncle. Can you please tell me what happened?" As soon as he introduced himself, the protective stance of the women relaxed, and they explained what happened.

They explained the highlights. Jim's head snapped back and forth as each woman interjected a part of the story. He felt as if he watched a fast-paced tennis match. Jim listened with focused attention to each woman's account until he heard the name of woman who had "attacked" Bree. He stopped them. "Wait, what? Ms. Harper? Are you sure?" They described Carson to a T, and he connected Bree's situation with the "gorgeous menace" that Carson had mentioned moments before. "Oh, shit."

❖

Bree exchanged contact information with Gwen, Suzanne, and her new friends. She was glad to know that Gwen and Suzanne lived in the area. The other women were close friends and visited the area often, so Bree hoped she would see them again as well. Bree was disappointed that she had to end their pseudo tour, but she was so worked up that she knew it would ruin the rest of their visit. Bree was beyond angry that her beautiful day had been destroyed by a crazed staff member with terrible social skills—albeit a crazy, captivating, and gorgeous staff member.

Jim followed as Bree headed straight to the car. She didn't want to disrupt his day any further, but she wasn't in the mood to continue her tour of the estate. She would have plenty of time in the future to wander the halls, if she ever managed to acquire a position in the house. "That woman was insane. People that rude should not work with the public." Bree offered her opinion as they walked along the trail to the parking area.

"I'm sure she was just having a bad day."

"A bad day?" Bree looked at him as if he had two heads. "That's not an excuse. Bad day or not, that was both unprofessional and uncalled for. Who is she, anyway? There is no way in hell she can be a guard or guide with that despicable attitude. If she is, she should be fired."

"I, uh, don't believe she is either," he said.

"Well, as long as she doesn't work in the curatorial department I couldn't care less. You know everyone. How do you not know a Ms. Harper?"

"I, um...I don't know. She must be new, maybe an intern?"

The idea that the wretched woman was an intern brightened her day a little bit. Interns were temporary, and positions were for a maximum of six months. So even if she was in the curator's department, it wouldn't have been for long. Bree couldn't imagine that such a Neanderthal was a preservationist or conservator. *It's unfortunate*, she thought. The dark-haired woman was stunning and stirred long-forgotten sensations deep inside Bree. She knew those eyes held passion and excitement, but Bree had overlooked the part labeled "crazy."

"Psycho," Bree said out loud, but mostly to herself.

"Oh, Breezy, maybe psycho is a bit exaggerated. She's not that...I mean, I don't think she's a psycho." Jim rubbed his forehead.

Bree disagreed. No sane person would have approached someone in public and berated them in such a way. Bree knew her mistake, and she also knew the damage that could be caused if everyone *accidentally* touched the displays. "Maybe if I'd ripped a swatch from the seat and stuffed it in my pocket I would've deserved such an inquisition. But it wasn't an act of purposeful vandalism, and the guard was more than skilled in how to advise and educate visitors on their mistakes."

Bree stared out the window and recalled how the woman had stared at her with an intense gaze from across the room—and how her heart had pounded in her chest. Bree's head had swirled as she prayed for something intelligent to say when she opened her mouth. Their eyes were locked in those moments, and Bree could see a heated passion that burned within them. It made her insides twist with excitement. She had felt a brief pang of disappointment when the guard drew her attention away from the approaching woman. Of course that was until the woman unleashed her barbarity. Bree was caught in an unfamiliar place between searing attraction and blind hatred. The idea of being attracted to such a jackass made her even angrier at the situation. How could she be so aroused by such a person? She detested herself and her inability to control her own hormones.

As Bree and Jim drove home, her thoughts jumped back and forth between the feelings of lust and disgust. The more she allowed herself to think about it, the thinner the line between them became. If Marion were with her she never would have had to experience any of it, not the fluctuating emotions or the embarrassing confrontation. But then again, if Marion were with her she would've been home, not in North Carolina.

CHAPTER SIX

Carson finished for the day and packed up her tools and equipment. She had focused on her work for the entire afternoon, and it did wonders for her frustration. What it didn't do was erase the image of a very alluring and feisty woman from her mind. Carson had shocked herself with the way she antagonized the guest on purpose. She was also surprised by how the other woman's emotions affected her. Once Carson discovered how to exploit those passions, she fed off them, and it aroused every part of her. She struggled to find a rational explanation for her actions because she considered herself far from antagonistic. She had always been proud of her avoidance of confrontation. Carson decided the most logical explanation for her actions was the hangover that raged through her and strangled her common sense.

Carson knew the chance was slim, but she decided she would call security the next morning to see if they'd collected the woman's name. The estate didn't make a habit of collecting offender names for such minor violations, but she had threatened Carson with punishment for her inappropriate actions, so there was a slight chance. While she cringed at the idea of her boss receiving word of the issue, she secretly hoped it had been reported. The thought of being punished by the woman who held her mind captive became more of a reward than a penalty.

"You're never gonna learn, are you?" Carson reprimanded herself for letting her appreciation for women cause such drama. Her stomach growled for food, and she dialed Jim's number on the way out to her truck. She figured his niece would be settled in by now, and a family dinner sounded like a fantastic idea after such a strange day.

"Hello?"

"Hey. How are your fingers doing?" Carson asked.

"Oh. Yeah. They're good. Fine." Jim was scattered in his response.

"Okay then. So, would you and Bree be interested in dinner tonight? If she's settled, of course." Carson's question went unanswered for several long seconds. "Jim? Hello?"

"Yeah. I'm here. You know, um...I don't know. I'll have to see if she's up for it."

"Um...okay." Carson felt that something wasn't right with him. He acted evasive, and that wasn't a trait of his, not with her. "I'm on my way home to change and such. Call me back after you talk to her."

"Okay. Yeah. I will," Jim said and hung up.

Something wasn't right, but Carson would wait for him to call her back. Any other time she would have blown up his phone with calls and texts. Once or twice in the past, she'd driven over to his house and made him talk to her. She didn't feel that this was a situation that called for such extreme measures. Carson assumed that having his niece back had his full attention, so she headed home. She'd just wait for him to call back when he got the chance.

❖

Jim hung up the phone without saying good-bye, and Bree recognized the oddity. "Who was that?" she asked.

"Huh? Oh, that? Carson."

"Oh, really? You should've asked if she was busy. We could go to dinner. I can't wait to meet her and talk to her about any job openings. Have you heard of any?"

Jim fidgeted in the driver's seat. "Oh, right. I should have. No. I haven't heard anything. I know Carson just got assigned the lead on the third-floor project, so she'll be looking to fill a couple of positions soon."

"That sounds great." Bree was confident she had more than what it would take to do the job. She was encouraged by the news. She would work at the Biltmore, of that she was certain.

Bree looked over at her uncle, who clenched his phone between the steering wheel and the palm of his hand. His eyes were focused on the road ahead, but she wasn't sure he saw anything in front of him. She waved her hand in front of his face until he blinked. "Uh. Are you okay?"

"Yeah, sweetheart. Okay, not exactly."

"Okay. I'm officially freaked out. What is wrong with you?" Bree was sick to her stomach. Her uncle was never so distracted. Bree's face drained of color as he looked over at her.

"It's not anything bad. Well, I'm not dying or anything like that."

"Well, that's…comforting." Bree was relieved when they pulled safely into their driveway and parked. It might not have been life threatening, but it had him so preoccupied she was sure the discussion should be had while at a complete stop. "Now tell me, what's going on?"

He turned in his seat and faced her. "Okay. Here's the thing. Today. What happened in the Damask Room—"

"Yeah. How could I forget?" Bree had thought of little else beyond the woman and her yelling. The feelings of disgust and lust resumed the battle in her stomach.

"Right. Well, the thing is, the woman. The one that 'yelled' at you—"

He was stalling, and it frustrated Bree. "Just tell me already, dammit."

"It was Carson. The woman was Carson."

Bree was stunned into silence. So many things ran through her head. She couldn't believe that Carson was both the gorgeous woman on the staircase with the crystal blue eyes that turned her insides to mush, and the horrible woman who verbally accosted her in front of an entire room of people. Bree sat in her seat for several moments as she tried to find her words. Her mind flashed between the sexy smile and the vicious mouth, both of which had induced very different physical responses earlier in the day. Bree inhaled deeply. "Okay. Let me get this straight. The woman, the one that condemned me for touching the chair is…Carson. Your Carson."

"Yes."

Bree's ears started to burn. "Carson. Your best friend? Oh my God, and my potential supervisor." Bree put her hand over her mouth and stared out the windshield of the truck.

"Bree, she's a good person. There has to be a reason for why she did that. That's not like her."

Bree looked over at him. "Wait, so when I told you it was Ms. Harper, you knew it was Carson, and you didn't tell me? You told me you didn't even know a Ms. Harper."

"Right. For this reason. I wanted the two of you to meet under different circumstances. I wanted you to be friends, and when you told me what happened I needed to figure out how to make it right. Needless to say, I didn't think of anything. Then Carson called and said she wanted to go to dinner and meet you. There isn't any way for me to avoid telling either of you."

"Carson doesn't know it was me?"

"No. I haven't told her yet." Jim rubbed his palms up and down the tops of his thighs.

"Did she tell you what happened?" Bree was curious to know what she had told her uncle without knowing who she was. Had she insulted her? Or maybe even complimented her in some way?

"No. She just said…she called you…never mind. It's not important." Jim tried to retract his statement.

"Oh, oh, no way. What did she call me?" Bree demanded.

"She might have called you a menace," Uncle Jim said as he shrank back from the impending explosion.

"Uh-huh, a menace. Really?" Bree's blood began to boil.

"And gorgeous," Jim offered.

"Gorg—What? She called me gorgeous?"

"'A terribly gorgeous rule-breaking menace.' But she said 'gorgeous' first." Jim smiled in consolation.

Bree had nothing more to say. She should be angry, but instead she was annoyed and flattered that Carson called her gorgeous. How was she supposed to work not with, but for, a hotheaded boss she found both infuriating and handsome in equal parts? There would be no way in the world anything good could come from such a situation. Bree felt lost. Things were turning into crap and she needed to regroup, and fast. "I'm gonna go in. Go to dinner with her. I have some things I need to take care of." Bree didn't wait for him to respond before she got out and headed up the hill to her house.

❖

"Shit," was all he could say as he watched Bree walk away. He fiddled with his cell phone before he dialed Carson's number. He should've known that his two girls wouldn't make things easy for him. Jim had hoped things would go a lot easier, and he now had less than twenty minutes to come up with something brilliant to get things back on track.

Jim waited at the table for Carson. He had just ordered a pitcher of beer when he saw her come in and waved her over. As she approached, she glanced around in search of the missing person.

"Jimbo. Where's Bree?" She patted him on the shoulder before she sat across from him.

"She wasn't feeling well," Jim lied.

"Oh. Well, that sucks." Carson expressed her true disappointment. "I hope she feels better soon. We should order her something and you can take it back for her."

"Uh, sure." Jim figured he wouldn't drag it out. "Well, that was a lie." He needed to tell Carson the truth, and he hoped it would work itself out naturally. He just needed to figure out where Carson stood after their encounter that morning. "In a way. We'll get back to that. Tell me what happened this morning. You didn't say much after you smashed my fingers to bits with the door." Jim raised his hand and flexed his fingers to show that they still worked in spite of the injury.

"Um. Okay. Nothing really. Some woman touched a chair in the Damask Room, and instead of waiting for security, I pursued her. I was going to confront her about it. I feel kind of bad about it now. I don't even know why I was so harsh with her. I kind of egged her on."

Jim could see the sincerity on Carson's face. He did know her very well, and just as he'd told Bree, it wasn't like her.

"Oh, I see." Jim hoped she would continue.

"Yeah. She had said it was an accident. I guess looking back at it, there were a lot of people, and she may have just been pushed forward and reached out to keep from falling. I do feel like a jerk. I'm going to call security in the morning to see if they got her name. I'd like to apologize for what happened."

"So why do you think you did it? It isn't like you."

"I don't know. I mean, I had a wicked hangover, I was running three hours late, and Becky was talking shit. But…Oh, man. I'd seen her on the stairs about fifteen minutes earlier, and I almost died. She was so beautiful. I saw her touch the chair so I followed her, but then…then I just stared at her. She was so angry, but it was gorgeous, and I couldn't help it."

Jim listened as Carson described Bree as gorgeous and beautiful. He puffed with pride. She was very beautiful to him, yet he had never heard someone else describe her with such ardor. He couldn't help but think that the cause might not yet be lost. "So, what if I told you I know who she is?"

Carson sipped her beer and eyed him skeptically. "And how would you know who she is?"

"Well, funny story—" he began to say.

"Oh my God. It was Bree. That was your niece. Wasn't it?" She set her beer on the table and crossed her arms.

"Yes. That was Bree and that's why she isn't here. I put two and two together this afternoon and told her on the way home after you called about dinner."

"What the hell, Jim? Why didn't you just tell me straight up?" she asked him, agitated by his method.

"Turns out I'm bad at revealing delicate information," he said as he smiled and raised his shoulders in submission.

"So, what you're telling me is that I not only yelled at my best friend's gorgeous niece, I accused a well-educated conservator of violating the number one rule of preservation? And I goaded her on in front of a room full of people just to satisfy my own voracious attraction? Geez, she was no doubt kicking her own ass about it the whole time." Carson covered her face with both hands. She was embarrassed for a variety of reasons.

"So, yeah. It seems that things may have gotten off to a rocky start," Jim said before he sipped his beer.

"Do you think, genius? Shit."

"Yeah, that's what I said."

CHAPTER SEVEN

W hy couldn't you be a painter? Or one of those glassblowing artists? There isn't a piece in this room that weighs less than a ton."

"Have you ever used a chisel on glass?" A short, fiery redhead motioned toward a workbench off to the side of the room. "Take a break then. We don't have to move it all today."

Kelli was Carson's best girlfriend and a very talented sculptor. She worked in a variety of mediums, including bronze, wood, and marble. Carson had a decent amount of artistic ability, but Kelli far outreached even Carson's wildest wish for talent. Kelli preferred to work in a very large scale, so it required both brute strength and industrial equipment to crate, move, and ship her pieces. Carson was the designated forklift operator in her spare time. She didn't mind because it meant she could spend quality time with Kelli. Plus, Kelli's studio was based out of the multi-use warehouse Carson owned and lived in, so it only made sense.

For the most part, quality time involved talks about Kelli's love life disasters and conquests, which most often contained drama at its highest levels. Kelli wasn't perfect, and anyone willing to deal with both her and her work would require incredible personal fortitude. They'd tried dating when they first met, but both of them realized early on they didn't have what the other needed, beyond mind-blowing sex. It was something they'd succeeded with keeping between them for about a year after they had broken up. Carson guessed that it was both the first and last time she'd had a successful friends-with-benefits arrangement. She had tried with several of her ex-girlfriends, but just like Becky, it hadn't worked out very well.

"So Becky went bat-shit crazy when you told her it was over, huh?" Kelli hollered over a large bronze casting of a semi-nude merman.

Carson admired the finely chiseled abs of the sea creature. "Not quite, but she was pissed. I should have expected it. I mean I did expect it. I don't know why I thought she would be able to overcome her feelings and have it work."

"I told you that, Car. She's what? Ten years younger than you, and I'd bet that you're her first real lesbian girlfriend. You know, outside of college crushes and curious straight chicks." Kelli rubbed a polishing cloth over the scaled bronze tail. Carson knew Kelli hated not being present when the movers uncrated the piece for the new owners. Kelli liked to see the faces of her clients when they first laid eyes on their commission. She said it was better than being paid. Carson agreed, but only to an extent.

"Bah, not my girlfriend. I know. I guess I just hoped it would work for both of us, that's all. I mean what's so hard about it? Good sex, an occasional dinner out, a movie, and more good sex. I don't understand the problem."

"Maybe you're too old for that. Maybe you're ready to find that someone to settle down with. Time to grow up?" Kelli jumped back out of the way as the workers lowered the crate over the sculpture. "Hey. Watch it," she yelled out.

Carson knew as well as anyone, including her regular work

crew, that if they didn't threaten to crate her in with the piece she would spend countless hours fussing over her creations. "Almost got you that time." Carson laughed. "I am grown up, and that is exactly what I'm trying to avoid. I have just about everything I could want—great job, amazing friends, beautiful home, and the ability to pick up and go if and when I want to. It's all I need."

Kelli walked toward Carson. "Yeah, that doesn't sound as lonely as you make it look."

"It's good—hey! I'm not lonely," Carson screeched as she threw a shop towel at Kelli.

"No?" Kelli ran a soft, seductive finger up Carson's arm.

"Stop that!" Carson jerked her arm away. "It's creepy. And no, I'm not lonely. I have you." Carson reached out for Kelli, who looked wounded.

"Oh no. It's creeeepy!" Kelli's voice was thick with sarcasm as she imitated Carson's words.

Carson didn't honestly think it was creepy. It was just that their relationship had changed over the years, and there was no longer any lingering sexual attraction between them. Carson adored her, and while she nurtured even Kelli's most questionable endeavors, they weren't compatible as a couple. There were a few times when she wished Kelli was her "one," because of how easy things worked between them. The idea was short-lived and they accepted that they were meant to be nothing more than devoted friends. Carson had tried to maintain friendships with a handful of her ex-girlfriends, but it was Kelli who had made it for the long term. That was okay with Carson, since Kelli's drama was about all she could handle in her life.

Kelli scrutinized the workers as they placed the lid on the crate and nailed it in place. When it was complete, she made several notations on the shipping documents on the clipboard she held. Carson was impressed. She was always certain that if Kelli put her mind to it, she would be a thriving artist. It seemed that once she'd gotten a taste of the success, her business took off. Every week, Carson moved more pieces than the week before. Considering that most of Kelli's work was of monumental size as well as price, Carson was happy to see that things remained strong for Kelli. It also helped that she didn't often turn down a commission, whether it be a headstone, a garden monument, or bronze portrait statue.

Carson wandered around one of Kelli's works in progress. Her current labor was being spent on a clay maquette of what was to become another colossal and breathtaking marble sculpture. The finished piece would be three times bigger than the model was. It was still incomplete, but Carson would bet that Kelli would have a handful of buyers eager to buy it even in its unfinished state. The image was of a young woman. Her frozen, distant gaze expressed sadness, and her flowing hair was suspended in motion around her innocent face. "What is this piece called?" she asked Kelli as she leaned in to get a closer look at the details in the clay.

"I don't know yet. Why?" Kelli strode over to the worktable where Carson stood.

"No reason. She looks so sad. Is she waiting for someone?" Carson saw a story written on the girl's face. At first glance it could have been one of sadness and loss, but beyond the hurt she could see the hope and longing in her eyes. A ping of emptiness echoed in her chest as the emotions that emanated from the statue pierced through her.

"I think so. By the look in your eyes, she isn't the only one."

Carson could have anyone anytime she wanted them. She was taken aback by the sentiment she drew from the inanimate object. But Carson knew she would never waste her time waiting around yearning for someone like that. She had to commend Kelli on her talent, because she had almost confused the sculpture's sentiments with her own. "Then let's get 'em on the truck, shall we?" Carson trotted off toward the forklift to get the pieces loaded onto the moving truck.

❖

Bree wandered in and out of the little shops and stores in the historic Biltmore Village. The neighborhood consisted of specialty establishments that sold things like one-of-a-kind custom jewelry, organic bath products, and collectible Christmas gifts. Bree always enjoyed weaving through the little boutiques, but it was the history of the buildings that interested her most. In addition to a massive chateau, George Vanderbilt had also constructed an entire town to house his estate employees and established recurring revenue for his self-sustained vision of Biltmore.

Bree picked up a local visitor paper and noticed several advertisements for the River Arts District, or RAD. The Asheville RAD was a developing art community on the other side of the French Broad River in an area once known for its vacant and derelict warehouse buildings. It had been adopted by local artists in an attempt to redevelop the area and establish a prominent and successful destination for artists and art lovers. Bree was intrigued. She decided to make her way across the river to see what there was to see. She was excited to visit the many working studios and on-site artist galleries housed in one area.

At first glance, Bree wasn't sure she was in the right place. However, once she realized that many of the studio fronts were simple in appearance, she noticed all the open overhead doors that exposed a variety of potential discoveries. Bree studied the map that marked the many studios in the area and found a public parking lot in a relatively central location. The weather was perfect for walking, and she didn't mind a little exercise, plus the happy sky with its cheerful white clouds begged for her company.

Bree was impressed by the life that emerged as soon as she had begun to walk along the street. "Open" signs and flags seemed to appear out of nowhere, as did a good number of people. She hadn't seen or noticed the liveliness or the activity when she drove into the area. It was almost magical. Visitors and artists mingled on the sidewalks and in the cafés and restaurants that dotted the thoroughfare. Bree meandered into the first building—a pottery studio and gallery. A potter hunched over a kick wheel as she threw a large urn-shaped vessel. The artist described her techniques to the handful of onlookers that circled around her. Like the group of people, Bree was mesmerized by the skill and ease of the potter's movements. Bree had attempted ceramics in college, and while she was proud of her pieces, she had never gotten the hang of the fluidity required for the art. She had made a couple of charming coil pots that her uncle displayed with pride and used as pen cups on his office desk. On her way out, Bree saw a sign that offered lessons and made a mental note to look into that for her spare time. The spare time that was about to increase now that the job in the preservation department was no longer on the table, thanks to Carson Harper.

Bree cursed at the thoughts of Carson during what had turned out to be a wonderful day. She forced herself to push the images of her from her head and continued on to the next studio on her map. The next building was a co-op of six artists housed in a bright multicolored building that was art in itself. Just from the look of the building Bree was excited to go inside. She knew there was no way she would get to all the studios with the time she had left in the day. The thought disappointed her, but she now had an excuse to return and spend even more time in the area on another day. Bree strolled in and out of the workshop spaces within the refurbished warehouse.

She looked at her watch and determined that she would have enough time for an iced coffee and one more studio before things started to close for the day. She ordered a coffee beverage and strolled along the sidewalk while she looked at her map. It pained her to walk by several other galleries as she searched for one in particular farther down the road. Bree looked around for the warehouse that should have been right in front of her. She saw a large moving truck but not much else. Not even a sign that indicated that she was getting close. She looked back at her map and sipped on her drink when she heard someone scream.

Bree looked up from her map just as something slammed into her and knocked her to the ground. The last thing she remembered was the slender red-haired woman who leapt toward her and a burst of warm liquid on her face before everything went dark.

CHAPTER EIGHT

Carson struggled to wrap her head around what had happened. She had just loaded the last crate onto the flatbed trailer and rounded the front of the truck when she heard Kelli scream. By the time Carson saw what Kelli shouted for she'd had barely enough time to hit the brakes. Had she waited another second to stop she wouldn't have been able to avoid hitting both Kelli and the woman she'd pushed out of the way. Carson watched in shock as Kelli tackled the woman and they both tumbled to the ground. She flinched when the stranger's head impacted the sidewalk. When she realized that Kelli moved, Carson dismounted the forklift and rushed over to them. Kelli crouched next to the unconscious woman and attempted to sit her up. Carson stopped her in case she had injured her neck when her head slammed into the ground. Carson checked the woman's pulse and was relieved when she felt a strong, steady beat.

Carson lay down next to the woman and whispered into her ear. She touched the strands of curly wet hair that were stuck across the woman's face. For a moment Carson feared the fluid might have been blood, but she was thankful when she detected the scent of coffee. As she moved the strands of hair from the woman's face, she gasped. "Oh, fuck."

"What? Fuck what?" Kelli said from somewhere close to Carson's shoulder. "Is she…Oh my God, she isn't…dead, is she? Oh my God."

Carson looked back toward Kelli, who had all but crawled onto Carson's side as she lay on the ground. "What? No. She isn't dead."

"Then what?" Kelli leaned in even closer.

"Kelli, back up. Go get me some water." Carson literally needed to get Kelli off her back so she could figure out what in the world she was going to do.

"Okay. Water. On it," Kelli said as she sprinted into the building.

Carson smoothed the hair off Bree's face as she whispered her name. "Hey. It's Carson. You've hit your head. If you can hear me, can you open your eyes for me?" Carson murmured to her. "Bree?"

Kelli came back at a run with a glass of water and stopped when she saw that Bree was still on the ground. "Carson, we need to call an ambulance. She should be awake."

"I know. My phone. Where's my phone?" she asked as she patted her shirt pockets.

Kelli reached into Carson's back pocket for her cell phone. "Here."

As Carson started to dial the emergency number, she heard Bree moan next to her. Carson paused momentarily to listen before she completed the call. "Bree? We're calling an ambulance. Don't move."

Bree moved her hand to the back of her head and pulled back blood-covered fingers. "Ouch. What the hell?" she said as she looked at her hand, more than a bit confused.

"Oh, damn. Okay," Carson said as she hit the send button on her phone. "Kelli, grab those paper towels on the lift. Okay, now come down here and put them on the back of her head."

As Carson and Kelli switched places, she said, "Don't let her get up."

Carson paced along the sidewalk as she described the situation to the dispatcher. She kept her eyes on them and watched as Kelli kept Bree conscious and calm until the paramedics could get there. She got off the phone with the operator and dialed Jim's number.

"Hey, Car. What's up, kiddo?" Jim said on the other line.

"Jim, it's Bree. She's had an accident. She's okay. The ambulance is on its way," Carson blurted out at him.

"What are you talking about? What happened? Where are you?"

"At my warehouse. Kelli's here. We were moving crates onto the truck. She hit her head. I tried not to hit her."

"Okay. Is she okay?" Jim was frantic.

"Yes. She's with Kelli. We're keeping her still until they get here."

"Okay, I'm on my way," he said as he hung up.

Carson heard Kelli tell Bree she didn't think it was a good idea as she walked back toward them. By the time she made it back to them, Kelli had helped Bree sit up to lean against the wall. Bree looked down at her shirt, which was covered in a large drying coffee stain. Carson couldn't help but think about how beautiful she looked even covered in dirt, blood, and coffee. Her heart tightened in her chest when it dawned on her that she'd almost run over Jim's niece.

Carson might have thought it a little sweet destiny had it not resulted in her nearly killing Bree with a forklift. It seemed to her that the two of them were destined to make each other's lives more interesting, or at least more dramatic. Carson could have stood for hours and stared at her, until a disheveled Bree looked up and saw Carson.

Bree's expression changed from confusion to recognition.

She glanced between Carson, Kelli, and the forklift. Her expression changed to something that Carson thought resembled surprise or maybe disbelief. When Bree spoke, Carson's stomach rose into her throat.

"Did you almost run me over with that thing?" Bree flinched from pain as she moved her head in the direction of the forklift.

"Not exactly," Carson's response was vague. In the distance, the sound of sirens broke the tension that materialized between them. She was thankful, in a way.

Carson turned toward the sound of the sirens and saw Jim as he ran up the sidewalk. She couldn't help but wonder if he had flown there. She walked toward him, and he slowed to a brisk walk that forced her to turn and walk with him as he passed. "She's okay. She's sitting up."

"Breezy. Hey, sweetheart, are you okay?" Jim stooped next to her and checked her for cuts and scrapes. Carson imagined he had done the same thing many times before when Bree was a child. As Bree and Jim talked, he looked at the wound on the back of her head and flinched. He was just about finished giving her a good parental once-over when the paramedics arrived and forced him to step back so she could be evaluated.

He turned toward Carson. "What the hell happened, Carson?"

Before Carson could answer, Bree shouted, "She tried to run me over with that damn forklift. That's what happened." Both Carson's and Jim's heads snapped around to Bree, who glared at her from between the two EMTs.

❖

Bree's head throbbed as the paramedics probed the back of her head where it had slammed into the ground. Bree refused to allow Carson to blame the situation on her in any way. She had already witnessed the way Carson twisted the details and forced the blame onto someone else before she heard the other person out. Jim and Carson stared at Bree. His expression was one of concern and interest, whereas Carson's was just as Bree would have expected, disbelief and denial.

"Um, she did what?" Jim looked back and forth between them. "Bree?" He waved a hand through the space between them.

Bree turned her attention to her uncle. As she started to repeat herself, Carson interrupted.

"Okay, wait a second. I certainly did not *try* to run you over, thank you very much. Although if Kelli hadn't pushed you out of the way I very well might have, but I did not *try*."

"Oh, right. Like you didn't see me on the sidewalk as you sped around on that thing without a bit of concern about anyone that could be around?" Bree flailed her arm for emphasis, but the EMT asked her to remain still, so she lowered her arm back down to her side.

"And what? You didn't see or hear a ten-thousand-pound forklift or the woman screaming at you?" Carson was agitated by Bree's accusations. "Kelli, can you help me out here?" Carson waved her over.

"Ma'am, we need to take your vitals and will need you to relax and be still for a moment," the male technician said.

Bree ignored him. "By all means, Kelli, please enlighten Ms. Harper as to what precisely happened." Something in Bree was further irritated when she thought that Kelli was Carson's girlfriend.

"Well, um, Carson was loading the last crate and was coming back around to bring the lift into the shop when I saw, Ms...um..." Kelli pointed at Bree.

"Whitley," both Bree and Carson said.

Kelli looked at them and then continued, "Right…Ms. Whitley, coming up the sidewalk. She was looking at a map, and I hollered at her, trying to get her attention. I don't think she heard me because she, you…" Kelli addressed Bree. "You kept walking, kind of oblivious. When you didn't stop, I ran toward you yelling, but by then I had no choice but to push you out of the way. I'm sorry," Kelli said with sincerity.

Bree listened and absorbed what Kelli had said until Carson spoke. "See. I think I'm due an apology. As a matter of fact, maybe even a thank you, since I technically saved your life."

"What? Are you serious?" Bree couldn't believe Carson played the *I saved your life* card. "You almost ran me over with a five-ton forklift, and since you stopped in time and called nine-one-one, you 'saved my life'? You are unbelievable." The paramedics pulled the stretcher to her side and helped her onto it.

"No. I checked your pulse, too."

Bree almost wanted to laugh at the way Carson had said it. If Bree hadn't been both pained and furious, she might have found Carson's innocent statement adorable. Coincidentally, Bree was now concerned about her appearance in front of Carson and her girlfriend. Before they strapped her onto the stretcher, she struggled to straighten her coffee-stained shirt and tame her wet and bloody mess of hair. When she realized she had primped herself for Carson, her fury returned, but for a very different reason; she was attracted to the egotistical, self-righteous, presumptuous woman, Carson Harper.

"Well, thank goodness for your Girl Scout honor, huh?"

"Wow. Maybe I should have just run you over," Carson mumbled.

"Excuse me?" Bree sat up on the stretcher and demanded that they stop before they put her in the vehicle. "Stop."

Everyone stood frozen, including the emergency response workers, afraid to move and detonate the bomb that had just been placed between them. All eyes were on Bree as they waited for her to speak, but it was Carson who did. Everyone's head snapped around at the sound of Carson's unexpected interjection.

"I said, maybe I should have run you over. Why are you so nasty? I didn't try to run you over, and as soon as it happened I was on the ground next to you, before and after I realized who you were. I called your uncle. I called nine-one-one. I checked your pulse and prepared to do CPR if I needed to. I brushed your hair out of your face and had Kelli get you water. I don't know why you're so damn mad at me for being nice and helping you. If it's about the other day, I'm sorry. I was having a bad day. I was out of line." Carson didn't wait for Bree to respond before she turned and disappeared into the building behind them.

Bree sat in silence on the stretcher and stared at Carson's retreating figure when her uncle approached her side. "Hey, kiddo. Let's go. I'm sure your head has got to be pounding, huh?" Bree knew he was trying to ease the tension, which was thick and hovered heavy in the air. It didn't help, but she appreciated it nonetheless.

Both she and her uncle were loaded into the back of the ambulance for the silent trip to the hospital. She felt fine, except for the ache in her head and the one in her gut. If she had thought there was any chance that she and Carson would be friends, she guessed it was all but hopeless now. Bree saw the disappointment on her uncle's face as they drove away from the studio.

CHAPTER NINE

Carson hated the tension that had developed between her and Jim. They'd always spent countless hours talking, joking, or nagging each other, yet, for two weeks, there had been a significant decline in their easy banter. Even so, they still spent a majority of their free time and breaks together. The biggest difference was that where there had once been an easy interaction, there was now awkward silence. It distressed Carson. She knew the reason for the change. What she didn't know was how to address it. The last thing in the world she wanted to do was hurt Jim any more than he already had been.

Since the accident at the studio, it was clear that Jim was caught in the middle of a situation that none of them had expected. Who would have known that his beloved niece and his best friend would border on being mortal enemies before they'd even been introduced? Carson didn't hate Bree. Carson found that Bree was on her mind more often than not since their encounter in the Damask Room. The thoughts had multiplied tenfold since the day on the sidewalk. Her opinion of Bree had changed more than a handful of times since the first moment their eyes met, and even still, Carson wasn't sure what her opinion was. All she knew was that she had never met someone who made her feel equal amounts of frustration, fury, and fervor simultaneously.

Carson stood near the mouth of the wisteria-draped arbors that ran along the wall of the upper Terrace Garden. As usual, she waited for Jim next to a fountain she called the Triton fish. It was one of Carson's favorite spots in the gardens. She had spent many hours seated on the bench between two of the marble busts that lined the corridor. She tried to think of her favorite time of day to visit. Carson found it next to impossible to choose between early fog-filled mornings or late sun-drenched afternoons. She spotted Jim as he approached and concluded she didn't have to choose. She would be content to enjoy it any way she could.

As had become their new custom in the previous weeks, Carson and Jim ambled along in silence toward the café. Yet on this day, Carson broke the silence. "Hey, do you mind if we go this way?" Carson asked as she pointed in the direction of the hearty shrub garden. Carson hoped that extra time spent wandering the long path would spark a much-needed conversation before they reached the café.

They walked for close to ten minutes in the quiet until Carson spoke again. "Okay, we need to talk about what's going on. It's seriously starting to irritate the shit out of me." She grabbed his arm and pulled him to a stop. "Are you not allowed to talk to me? This all feels very *my mommy told me I couldn't be friends with you anymore*, and it's getting a little frustrating."

Jim let out a chuckle, and the tension eased somewhat. "No. My *mommy* didn't say anything of the sort. And neither did Bree if that was going to be your next question. She's my daughter, not my mother."

"I mean, I know she's your daughter, at least more than

I would ever be, but I still consider you very much like my father and one of my very best friends. In ten years, there hasn't been anything we couldn't talk about, even if you are old as dirt." Carson's laugh was uneasy. She hoped he would join in like always. After what seemed like hours, Jim laughed at her joke. For the first time in weeks, she was hopeful that things would return to normal.

"I had you there for a sec, huh?"

Carson realized his exaggerated delay of laughter was his own cruel joke. "You asshole!" she said as she punched him in the arm.

"Ow. Damn." He rubbed the frog from his bicep and then put his arm around Carson's shoulders. "No worries, kiddo."

"So we're cool? Us?" Carson leaned in to his hug.

"Of course."

Where the shrub garden ended, the famous azalea garden began. The azaleas covered roughly fifteen acres of land with over a hundred varieties of native and non-native plants. When they were in full bloom, the sight was overwhelming. "So, how is she?" Carson didn't know if they would ever be friends, but she wanted Jim to know that she would get along with Bree, for him. Carson didn't know how she would convince Bree that she wasn't a self-centered jerk or how Bree would convince her that she wasn't a feisty, defensive brat.

Of course that was if Carson's initial opinion of Bree proved incorrect—which Carson had no real doubt it would be. Something inside Carson told her that things would change between them; she just didn't know when or how. Either way, she was excited to think there would be another encounter.

"She's good." Jim's hesitation to answer the question was evident.

"Good to hear. Did everything with her head get taken care of?" As soon as Carson said it she realized how it might have sounded, and she laughed. She was relieved when Jim laughed, too.

"Yes. A few stitches that she got out yesterday, and the doctor said everything looked normal. I asked her to get a second opinion," he said, and they both struggled to keep a straight face. "No, really. She's fine. She started training with Barbara on Monday."

Carson was confused. "Barbara who?"

"Barbara Williams with guest relations. Barbara is short-staffed with the new tour options, and she thought Bree would be perfect for now." Jim and Carson entered the walled garden area and she heard Jim's stomach growl.

"Wait." Carson stopped and made Jim do the same as she grabbed his arm. "Jim, she has her master's degree in art conservation. Why the hell would she give that up to play tour guide?" Carson was a mix of emotions. "Please tell me you're kidding."

"I'm not kidding. She's an excellent tour guide. She knows this place inside and out, and she enjoys it," Jim said matter-of-factly.

"I understand that. But what about my positions? I'm going to be hiring soon, remember? I mean, I know we haven't gotten off on good terms, but we're both professionals. Did she not think that I could overcome our differences and be a professional? Is that it?" There it was. Carson should have guessed. Bree was blaming her for ruining her career and implying that she wouldn't hire her based on some nonexistent personal vendetta.

"Carson, wait. That has nothing to do with it," he said.

"Really? She told you that?" Carson crossed her arms and waited for his answer.

"No…not exactly." She attempted to interrupt. "Wait. Will you let me finish before you continue your tantrum?"

Carson huffed but remained quiet. "Barbara needed help. You aren't ready for that project to start yet and therefore aren't hiring right this moment. Bree is bored. She moved here to work at Biltmore and start her life over. Sitting in the house alone is not going to get her through things. It might not be just as she had planned it, but she has to do something." Jim turned and continued toward the café and left Carson to reflect on his words.

Carson felt like she had been picked up off the floor mid-flail and set upright with a smack on the bottom. He was right, and she was an asshole. She followed him into the café.

❖

A few days earlier as Jim performed his various inspections, he had been approached by Barbara. Jim had known Barbara Williams for several years and they always had an easy rapport and spoke often. So it wasn't a complete surprise that she seemed to go out of her way to talk to him when they were in the same area. However, this time Barbara didn't make her usual small talk about the staffing changes or ask innocuous personal questions. She approached and handed him a completed job application. Before he could ask her why she'd handed it to him, he noticed the name at the top, *Bree L. Whitley.*

Barbara explained that she had received the application the day before and that she was almost as surprised as he was. She knew Bree very well, as did just about everyone who worked in the house. Barbara also knew Bree had gone to school to be a conservationist and her life's goal was to return and one day become chief conservator at the Biltmore. So Jim understood the look of confusion in Barbara's eyes as she stood and waited for Jim to confirm Bree's identity. It appeared that

Bree had applied for a tour guide position in secret, from him anyway. He acknowledged that Bree was the applicant. Bree was an adult and if she wanted to be a tour guide, he would stand behind her in that decision. He stated that she would be perfect for the position if Barbara wished to hire her.

Jim knew why Bree had applied for the job instead of waiting for a call from the preservation department, and the reason upset him. He wanted nothing more than for his girls to get along. But it seemed that neither his nor Bree's plans were going to come to them without difficulty. When Jim got home that day he detoured by Bree's place first. He vowed to support her. He just wanted to have a rational explanation first. Bree was both goal-oriented and methodical, and while most of her decisions made sense to him, he needed a more detailed justification to understand the impulsiveness of this one. Plus, Bree would always be his little girl, so if she decided to begin making rash choices he preferred that she at least discuss them with him. Either way, regardless of what he said, she would do as she wished.

He pressed the doorbell and waited for Bree to answer. He heard her shout from inside, "Come in. I'm in the office." Jim went in and then down the hall to the office. Bree's office consisted of a drafting table, a large computer desk, and what seemed like thousands of books.

Jim sat on the couch across from Bree, but he didn't sit back. Instead he leaned forward and rested his chin in his hand. Bree looked up from her computer screen and laughed. "Uh-oh." He knew that she knew his mannerisms well enough to read his mind most of the time, so it didn't take long before she talked.

"Yes, I applied for the guest services position. No, I didn't tell you, and no, I don't know why. I figured it would take longer than twenty-four hours for you to find out, though."

She offered all the answers without any of the questions. Jim couldn't help but smile.

"Okay then. I guess I just figured you would have at least mentioned it to me. I wouldn't have tried to change your mind." Jim was interrupted by a scoff from Bree. "Okay, I would have offered my opinion that you wouldn't have listened to anyway. But can you tell me why the hasty decision to be a guide instead of waiting for the other position?" He braced himself for the answer.

"There are several reasons, I guess. And it's not such a hasty decision. You and I both know I don't need to work. I love what I do, and ever since I could remember I've wanted to be a conservator at the Biltmore, but I know how hard it is to get in there. Even with your connections. I never once hesitated when I made the final decision that it was time to come home. I had hoped that a position would open up quickly and much of my plan rested on the possibility, but even a control freak like me knows things don't always go as smoothly as you might want them to."

As always, Jim was mesmerized by her controlled spontaneity; even though her plan seemed rash, it was still a reasonable option. "So, this has nothing to do with Carson?" He knew it did; he just didn't know if she would admit it.

"Honestly, yes, in a way," Bree said. "While I find myself easy to get along with and very much a people person, Carson Harper is proving to be quite a challenge for me. I mean, she's so…difficult? Egotistical? Abrasive maybe? We've met twice, that's it, and both times ended with me wanting to punch her right in the nose." Jim looked at her in shock. Bree wasn't the violent type, and he didn't think she had ever talked about physically assaulting another person before. "I know, right? She's infuriating. And I just don't think a working relationship would be possible. Right now anyway."

Bree wasn't finished so Jim leaned back into the couch and waited for her to continue. It was apparent she had contemplated her feelings and the situation for a while. He believed it was best if she continued and got it all off her chest.

"I know what she means to you. I'm so sorry I'm interfering with your friendship."

Jim stopped her and went to her side. "Bree, my love. You're my precious girl. You always come first with me. I love Carson like a daughter, but you're my family, okay?"

"I know. But I saw the disappointment on your face that day at the studio and—"

"No. Just stop. I understand why you've made these decisions, and I admire all of your reasons. I think you'll make a fantastic guide for a day, a week, or a year. I know Barbara is beside herself with joy at the idea of having you working for her." Jim smiled to ease the tension that had built.

"I'm excited about it. All the fun and none of the stress."

"Well, that's if you even get the job. I haven't given the okay yet. It is I with the power to determine your future. Bwah ha ha." Jim gave his best and worst evil laugh.

Bree put her hands under her chin, widened her innocent eyes, and gazed up at him. "Please, Uncle Jiiiim?" she cooed.

"Dammit! My kryptonite. Fine, you win…this time."

"Either I've finally perfected that or you're getting weak as you get older." Bree squealed and jerked her shoulders up to her ears as he squeezed the back of her neck. Bree hated to be tickled, but Jim couldn't resist it. He enjoyed how funny it was when Bree begged him to stop while she tucked her head into her body like a turtle.

CHAPTER TEN

Jim saw Bree near the base of the staircase and watched as she paced back and forth in the small alcove beneath the chandelier. She was in deep concentration but her nervousness was clear. She no doubt reviewed the hundreds of facts and figures that every good guide at Biltmore would know. Jim knew Bree could have fired off any number of those facts with ease, in addition to the handfuls of other lesser known details she'd learned over the years. She was a wealth of data and information, especially when it came to her second home. He continued to watch her mumble and pace from a safe distance on the other side of the Winter Garden. He wasn't about to disturb her as she prepared for her final test.

Bree had trained no more than a week, so they were both surprised when Barbara requested that Bree participate in the next mock tour testing. It was common for new guides to study and train for weeks before they were given the opportunity to take the final exam. While Jim knew that Bree was heads above the *newbs*, Barbara had never been one to circumvent the rules or traditions of the house, even for family. Barbara always had a fondness for Bree while she grew up in the shadows of the house. Jim had assumed that she, like many of the other women, had fostered Bree as one of their own in the wake of her mother's tragic death.

Jim and Bree had a very open and honest relationship, but there were some things he couldn't teach her by experience. On more than one occasion, he'd even asked Barbara about how to address certain feminine topics. While Jim had always tried his best to provide Bree with what she needed to know, he never turned away trusted advice from Barbara. It had been many years, and Jim wondered if Barbara remembered the time she had commandeered the discussion about puberty.

Jim had thought he prepared rather well, considering all his knowledge was gleaned from library books and medical pamphlets. One day, he brought them all to her office along with a carefully prepared lecture. Jim wanted to make sure he had all his facts right in a complete and helpful manner. As soon as he set out his documentation, complete with body diagrams and instruction sheets, Barbara burst into tears and laughter. She all but begged him to allow her to talk to Bree about it. While he was more than capable of having the talk with his niece, he was far from disappointed when Barbara requested permission to do it instead. It still made him laugh to remember both his elaborate setup and her amused response to it.

Bree still pointed at invisible sights and waved her note cards in sweeping gestures through the air. He smiled at the thought of how seriously she took everything she did.

"She could've been an actress," he heard a woman say from behind him. He turned around. Barbara stood a few feet away and watched Bree conduct her tour to her imaginary guests.

"Yes, she always has been quite dramatic," he said. They both laughed at the truth in the statement.

"I don't know what she's so nervous about. She knows this entire estate better than you and I both." Barbara's statement wasn't exaggerated. After all, Bree had been mentored and tutored by almost every department head and employee in the house since she was eight years old.

"No kidding. It wouldn't surprise me if she became director of museum services one day. Although, at this rate, I don't think she even cares, just as long as she's here." They both watched her as she spun in a dramatic motion and all but slammed into an unsuspecting sightseer. Jim cringed. "Oh geesh. Is coordination on that test of yours?"

"No, it isn't. Which, by the looks of it, is a good thing." Barbara said.

They exchanged a glance that held for a brief moment longer than Jim had expected. He was thankful when he heard a familiar voice break the unexpected connection.

"Jeeems! Where've you beeeen?" Carson shouted in a long, drawn-out, and exaggerated Southern accent.

"What are you yelling for, you nut?" Jim asked Carson.

"I've been looking all over for you. Hi, Barbara."

"Hey, Carson."

"I've been right here, talking to Barbara and watching Br—people." Jim tried to avoid the mention of Bree in front of Carson and vice versa. It helped ease the tension. The problem was that Carson wasn't as dumb as he wished she was sometimes, and she spotted Bree across the room.

"People? Or person?" Carson asked as she stared at Bree while she paced. "What is she doing exactly?" Carson said as she moved past them but hugged close against the wall like a chameleon.

Jim was sure he wasn't the only one who had noticed the look in Carson's eyes when she spotted Bree. He cast a curious look at Barbara, who raised an eyebrow at him. Confirmed, it wasn't just him. He smiled, and something inside him melted just a little bit. They both looked back at Carson, who still hugged the wall in silence. "Riiiight," Barbara said louder than necessary in a vain attempt to bring Carson back down to earth. "So, the mock tour test starts in thirty minutes. Do you want to help out and be a Biltmore guest for a while?" Barbara looked at Jim but spoke loud enough for Carson to hear. "I don't think Bree would mind."

Carson's head nearly spun off her shoulders. Barbara smiled and Jim covered his mouth as he tried to muffle his laughter. Carson didn't seem to notice. "A tour? I'll help. I can spare a couple of hours," Carson said as she looked at Jim for his agreement.

Barbara looked at Jim, who still struggled to appear reserved and not give away that he just witnessed Carson's attempt to leap into Barbara's arms at the invitation. He hoped that Bree didn't have the exact opposite reaction when they both showed up for her test. He hesitated to accept the request, but in the end decided against his better judgment. "Okay. I'm sure she won't mind at all."

"Sweet. I'm gonna go get ready…I mean go let Beth know where I'll be in case they need me. I'm sure they won't. Cool. See you in a few." Carson bolted toward the Billiard Room through the door marked "Staff Only."

Barbara looked back at Jim with a knowing smile on her face, to which he responded with a shrug. "What?"

"Cute. Just make sure it doesn't distract Bree from her test." She stroked his arm and walked away.

❖

Bree stood in front of the bathroom mirror and adjusted her blouse. She looked at her reflection and took a long, calming breath. She had no idea why she was so worked up about the tour. She knew more about the entire estate than even the experienced guide they'd partnered her with the week before. While Jennifer was knowledgeable and proficient in the fundamentals of the house, she lacked the familiarity and the fondness for the nuances that made Biltmore an extraordinary piece of history.

One of the reasons why Bree enjoyed guided tours was the feeling of being treated to something special. She wanted something above and beyond what she could get from renting an audio guide or opting for a self-guided approach. So for Bree, offering what seemed liked hidden secrets or lesser known facts gave her audience a more personal and tailored experience. It was when she strayed from the studied statistics that she questioned her preparedness. Personal experiences and stories were more prone to be misinterpreted or misrepresented and therefore caused her to second-guess her strategy for the mock tour.

Bree glanced at her watch. There was no more time to worry. The tour started in five minutes, and she was either ready or she wasn't. In the end, she knew the facts, and while it was not her particular style, if she relied strictly on those facts she would get through the test without fail.

Two groups congregated just outside the main entry as several anxious individuals crowded around Barbara. Bree recognized them as her fellow trainees who no doubt harassed Barbara with last-minute questions about what they should expect over the three or more hours to follow. As Bree headed over she glanced toward the second group of people. She recognized more than a handful of Biltmore staff, including her uncle. She smiled. She was just about to call his name when another voice beat her to it. Bree's stomach leapt into her throat and the blood rushed in her ears the moment she spotted Carson, who walked toward Jim and the rest of the group. "You've got to be kidding m—" Her body came to a crashing halt as she collided with a brick wall.

It wasn't until he reached down to pick her up off the ground that Bree noticed the "wall" was in fact her friend Alan, a six-foot-four mass of muscle. He scooped his hand under her arm, and she struggled to her feet as she prayed that no one saw what happened. Once she got to her feet, a quick inventory of eyes revealed that everyone around her watched as she dusted the dirt and debris from her butt. To her dismay, those eyes included both her uncle's and Carson's. "Just freaking fantastic," Bree mumbled to herself.

Bree was relieved when Barbara took the break in everyone's attention to announce the commencement of the mock tour test. She brought both groups together and explained the process. The trainees and the group would make their way through the entire estate. They would stop in every room and area that was included in the tours available to guests. Once in the room, Barbara would randomly select one of the student guides to give a brief lecture on that room. The details of their lectures were required to include facts about the furniture, history, décor, and any significant information that might be of interest to the visitors. Just as in real time, each dissertation would conclude with an opportunity for the guests to ask questions.

Barbara scanned the group for her first victim. As her eyes perused each of them, Bree reviewed everything she knew about the exterior of the Biltmore property. The dull throb in her backside and Carson's unexpected presence had her scatterbrained. Bree was grateful when Barbara chose the brick wall, Alan, as first up.

Bree didn't even have to see her to know that Carson's gaze was focused on her. The heat from her steel blue gaze proved to be a far greater distraction than her sore bottom. The group wandered through the first-floor rooms. They followed the self-guided tour map. Bree had hoped to be selected for the library, but she had no way to predict which areas Barbara would combine or how random her guide choices were. When they reached the Tapestry Gallery, it was Bree whom Barbara chose.

Bree didn't mind. She enjoyed the room, most of all the tapestries. The first time Bree ever came to Biltmore, her uncle introduced her to a group of conservators that had just begun work on a multiyear project to restore and preserve the sixteenth-century Flemish textile works. Bree remembered that she had been unimpressed by the concept until she saw the great care and precision that went into the protection of the tapestries.

As expected, Bree listed off various facts and figures about the ninety-foot long Tapestry Gallery and the portraits by John Singer Sargent and Boldini. As Bree described the original pieces purchased by George Vanderbilt in 1887 during a trip to France, she watched the glossy looks of boredom that crept over the eyes of her audience. Even the most dedicated amateur historian could absorb just so much impersonal data. Even her uncle looked as if he was a wild animal trapped in a cage too small. Bree had both seen it and felt it before. When the guests got bored, they lost focus and the guide lost control. Bree decided to take a different approach.

"When I was a child, my uncle brought me here to the Biltmore. I got the super-secret, behind the scenes tour because this is where he worked." Bree looked at her uncle with great fondness. "I was nine and the technicians were mere weeks into what would become a five-year endeavor to restore and preserve these tapestries." Bree told her story and interlaced facts and memories that included how they custom-built an eighteen- by twenty-five-foot wash bath in order to hand scrub and clean the pieces. All eyes were on her, including those of her fellow trainees; each person seemed to be as enthralled in her memory as she was, including Carson.

Bree stared at her. She was unable to look away from the deep and penetrating gaze. She was paralyzed and felt as if her entire body was on fire. Bree didn't realize she had stopped speaking until Barbara asked if anyone had any questions. Barbara's interruption allowed Bree to break free from Carson's hypnotic stare. "Yes. Questions? Anyone?" Bree coaxed. When Carson appeared to make a move to raise her hand, Bree was saved by Barbara's announcement that they were ready to move on. She used the distraction as her opportunity to escape. Bree shuffled between her classmates and through the doorway ahead of the group, out of range of Carson's searing eyes.

CHAPTER ELEVEN

Three hours after they'd begun, the group and its guides approached the end of the testing. Bree's legs had begun to scream from the constant standing and swaying she'd done for the last few hours. She felt very good about her performance, but the one takeaway was the need to work on leg stamina. Bree had spent the final forty-five minutes staring at each bench, chair, or even protective railing as a place to lean her ass against, even if just for a second. Of course she never did, and it had become the only thought in her mind.

After the last trainee finished his presentation, no one offered any questions. It was clear that everyone was ready to be dismissed for lunch. Much to everyone's obvious relief, Barbara announced the conclusion of the examination. She advised them to meet back in an hour, and the group dematerialized. This left Bree, Barbara, Uncle Jim, and Carson, who stood like random chess pieces scattered on a board. Barbara and Jim conversed with each other while Bree and Carson stood in awkward silence, desperate not to make eye contact.

At least that was Bree's intention. Carson seemed far more confident in her decision to stay planted in one spot and was determined not to shy away if Bree's eyes met hers. Bree refused to allow herself to look into Carson's eyes. They seared through into her soul, and Bree felt exposed and out of control. Her entire body burned under Carson's unabashed gaze.

Just before her legs turned to ash and crumbled beneath her, Jim called her name. "Thank God." She looked in his direction as he and Barbara approached her. Bree's legs tingled. Even if she had been certain that the sensation was due to the countless miles she'd walked, she didn't disregard the effect Carson was having on the solidity of her legs. She feared that if she was unable to sit soon, she would topple over.

For weeks, Bree had attempted to overcome the awkwardness from the forklift incident, and there was no way in hell she would let Carson rescue her if her legs gave out. Bree took another look in Carson's direction and she still had not moved an inch. She continued to stare at Bree with an expression she could only have described as ravenous. Before she could do anything to prevent it, Bree's face burned red. "Shit."

"What was that?" her uncle asked as he stopped in front of her.

"What? Oh nothing. My legs are killing me. I need to sit down somewhere."

"Why don't we go get some lunch, and we can all sit down?" Barbara offered.

"That sounds great," Jim said. "How's that sound to you, Car?" He looked back over his shoulder to where Carson still stood.

Bree's stomach leapt into her throat. "Oh, I'm sure she needs to get back to work," she said in a definitive tone.

They looked at Carson and waited for her answer. Carson looked from Barbara to Jim and then to Bree. She raised an eyebrow and smiled wryly. "Nope. I'm very much available… for lunch."

"Great," Jim said.

"Yeah, great," Bree mumbled as they all turned in the direction of the Library Lounge restaurant.

Barbara and Jim chatted about a random newspaper article they'd both read earlier that day. Bree couldn't even string coherent syllables together with Carson just a few feet behind her. She didn't even need to turn around to know just how close Carson was. Bree heard her deep and steady breaths, but she also felt Carson's eyes as they traveled over every inch of her body. Bree wanted to break out into a run ahead of them, but her legs wouldn't comply.

She closed her eyes and considered making an abrupt stop so that Carson's body would collide with hers. Bree wondered how the arcs of Carson's breasts and stomach would feel pressed against the curves of her back. When a sudden pain shot through her foot, her eyes flew open. "Shit." Bree extended her arms out in front of her as she prepared for impact, but her forward motion was stopped, and she hovered almost magically above the floor in front of her. Then, in an instant, she was spun around and pulled up against Carson's chest without a breath of air between them.

Bree couldn't move. She stared into Carson's smoldering eyes and prayed that she didn't let her go because she would have ended up in a heap of goo on the tile. Bree squeezed the flexed shoulders that held her securely upright. They were tight and so steady. With lust burning in her eyes, Carson smiled at Bree who snapped out of her trance and thrust herself out of Carson's arms. Her legs supported her, and for that she was grateful.

Bree was flooded with emotion. She was aroused, embarrassed, and remorseful. *What are you doing? Why are you having such a hard time staying on your feet around this woman?* Bree recalled the first time she'd seen Marion and how she had made a fool out of herself in front of her as well. The difference was that she couldn't remember having been quite as aroused as she was with Carson.

Bree felt a twinge of guilt that she was reacting in such a powerful way toward someone else for the first time since Marion. She couldn't remember the last time that she even looked at another woman, let alone found herself on the edge of a burning attraction. She knew that she would never love another woman the way she loved Marion, so she had no idea why she was getting herself all worked up over this one. And in the back of her mind she still held on to the tiniest fleck of hope that Marion would find her and come home.

Bree's self-flogging was interrupted when she witnessed something unexpected. Her uncle brushed his hand over the small of Barbara's back as they proceeded through the doorway. Never in her life had she seen him make any sort of romantic or flirtatious gesture toward another woman. All of a sudden, she was so full of hope that she felt as if she floated above the floor. It was a sign she'd never expected, but one that was too hard to ignore.

Before they were even seated, Bree anticipated the awkward and strained conversation. She expected to spend an hour staring into her water glass while she prayed for the powers that be to either save her, kill her, or both. Yet that wasn't the case, not at all. To Bree's complete surprise, lunch proved to be much more interesting than she had expected. They laughed and joked, and at one point Bree even tolerated the group's playful teasing over her collision with Alan's back. Although afterward, Bree joked and demanded that the incident be stricken from everyone's future comedic repertoire, at least until the bruise on her ass went away.

Bree watched how Carson interacted with her uncle. Their friendship was so easy. It was obvious that they were very close, quite similar to the way Bree and Jim had always been. Bree figured out why he had wanted his girls to get along. Bree could see that she and Carson had very much in common and were rather compatible. *In a strictly platonic sort of way, of course.* "Like sisters." It hadn't been her intention to say the last part out loud.

"You like sisters?" Carson said with a wink. "I'm not sure how that relates to the recent discovery of a new species of snapping turtle, but it's good to know."

"That's not what I meant. I was just observing our similarities, if you must know. And I concluded that we're like sisters." Bree didn't see the point in denying what she had said. Plus she lacked the quick wit she needed to save herself.

"Sisters?" It was obvious that Carson expected further explanation.

"Well, yeah, I guess. You and I have a lot in common it seems, and of course it takes a special kind of person to deal with him." Bree gestured across the table toward Jim.

"I can agree with the last part, but it's the first part I want to hear more about." Carson leaned in closer and raised an eyebrow at Bree.

Bree felt her stomach cartwheel. Carson's Caribbean blue eyes sparkled with curiosity and desire. "I, well, I don't know offhand." Bree scoured her mind for anything except for the one discernible thought about how close Carson's body was to hers.

"I'll just let you think about it. Let me know what you come up with." Carson sat back in her seat but didn't take her eyes off Bree's.

Bree could've kissed the waiter when he appeared out

of nowhere and broke the spell Carson had cast upon her. Once they were all engrossed in their desserts, the tension disappeared, and they resumed their comfortable familiarity.

❖

Carson loved to watch Bree's mouth move. When Carson thought about it, there wasn't anything that Bree did that Carson didn't like. She'd grown to adore the more questionable moments they'd shared, including the one on the sidewalk in front of her warehouse on that memorable day. They finished up their lunch, and Carson found that she wished to spend the rest of the day at the table. She knew it was impractical, yet she was still disappointed when they got up and left the restaurant.

The four of them stood in the hallway and said their polite good-byes with hugs and handshakes. When Bree reached out for her hand, Carson hesitated. Her reason was twofold. For the most part it was because she wasn't ready to say farewell, but also because Carson wasn't sure what would happen when they touched. Carson grabbed Bree's hand; a simple handshake felt too impersonal, but swooping her into a kiss was quite the opposite. Instead, Carson ignored the sirens that blared in her head and brought Bree's hand up to her mouth.

She leaned down and brushed her lips against Bree's soft hand. She locked her eyes with Bree's. Carson watched as Bree's lips parted slightly, and she heard a sharp intake of breath. As Carson's lips touched Bree's hand, she smelled the enticing aroma of crisp perfume and wondered if the rest of Bree smelled just as delicious. She knew it did. She stood and lowered Bree's hand. Carson smiled. "Thank you."

Bree just stared at her with her beautiful face flushed pink. Carson felt Jim's hand on her arm. When that failed to draw her attention away, he squeezed. The unexpected and crushing handgrip caused her to look over at him. He nodded in the direction behind them. It was a clear signal that meant it was time to return to work or at least to stop manhandling his daughter. Carson smiled again. "It was my pleasure, Ms. Whitley. I hope we can do this again soon."

Barbara also interjected. "Okay. Thank you for lunch, you two. We really should be getting back to the group. It wouldn't look very good for the teacher and her prize pupil to both be late." She winked at Jim and tapped Bree on her arm. After they turned and walked away, Carson followed after Jim in the opposite direction.

"What the hell was that, Carson Harper?" Jim grumbled to Carson as they headed down the hallway.

"What was what?" Carson's response may have been nonchalant, but she knew exactly what he had meant.

"You know what. I'm talking about the eye contact and the flirty smiles and the...hand kissing. Is this 1945? Do people even do that anymore?"

"I don't know what *people* do. But I thought it was a perfect thing for *me* to do at that moment." Carson looked at him. She didn't even attempt to hold back the excitement that consumed her inside and out. She raised her eyebrows, and the smile disappeared.

"What? What's wrong?" Jim asked, concerned.

Carson didn't answer; she just reacted. She took off back toward the restaurant and hoped Bree was still in the hallway. At first, Carson didn't see her, but once she was past the restaurant, she spotted Bree and Barbara as they approached the stairs. "Bree," Carson yelled, a little louder than necessary, and Bree turned around. "Ms. Whitley," she said a bit quieter the second time as Bree looked at her with surprise.

"Hi. Is everything okay?"

Carson slowed to a stop before her. "Yes. I was just wondering if you'd be interested in going out this weekend or sometime?" Carson asked.

"Oh. Well, I don't know if that's—"

"Just as friends. You know, because we have so much in common and all," Carson offered to help in Bree's decision.

"Friends? Really?" Bree asked.

"Absolutely. Here's my number. Text me and we can figure out what we can do…as friends."

"Oh. I guess…I think I can do that." Bree smiled.

If not for her bones, she'd have melted at Bree's feet. "Excellent. Soon then." Carson watched Bree when she turned and walked away. It took every bit of reserve she had not to skip back down the hallway to where Jim leaned against the wall with crossed arms.

As Jim stared at her, she battled to keep the smile at bay. When she got to him she could no longer control it. She beamed and jabbed a few playful punches at him. "She said yes." Carson said as she grabbed his shoulders. "Well, she took my number anyway."

"Just like that?" Jim asked her. "She doesn't even like you. How did you do that?"

"I have no idea. None whatsoever, Jimbo. But that doesn't matter because she said yes." Carson grinned and punched Jim on his arm.

"Unbelievable."

Carson figured Jim would have been more pleased at the sudden turn of events. Yet Jim showed little sign of it as he walked ahead of her in silence. As long as he didn't have a problem with it, which he most definitely would have mentioned, she would just wait for him to come around when he wanted to talk.

She and Jim went their separate ways when they got

downstairs to the workspace. Carson had five hours of work to catch up on before she left for the weekend. A price she would be glad to pay again to spend more time with Bree. With the sharp memory of Bree's stunning smile ingrained into her mind, Carson stuck in her headphones and settled in for a long night's work.

Chapter Twelve

Carson lay on her back on top of a giant block of marble. She swung her legs as they hung off the end of the stone. Carson pressed a button on her phone and checked to see if she had any texts. It hadn't rung or vibrated in the three minutes since she had last checked it, but she couldn't help herself. It was the proverbial watched pot of the technology era. She resisted the urge to ask Kelli to send a test text. Carson pushed the phone into the front pocket of her jeans and then sat up. "Ugh," she grunted.

"Still nothing?" Kelli said as she peeked out from behind an enormous glob of modeling clay.

"Nope. Nothing."

"Well, I wouldn't worry about it. She's probably just busy. Not everybody has time to just sit around in a warehouse drinking beer." Kelli looked around, having just realized she had misplaced her own beverage.

Carson spotted the bottle and picked it up. As she handed it to Kelli, her phone chimed. Before Kelli had gotten a firm grip on the bottle, Carson let go and scrambled for her phone. At the same moment that she stuck her hand into her pocket, the glass smashed onto the concrete floor. Carson looked at Kelli, whose hand was still positioned as if she held an invisible drink. "Oops."

"Wow. You get that," Kelli said as she gestured to Carson's phone, "and I'll get the broom." She shook her head and wiped her hands on her apron.

Hey Carson, this is Bree. -B

Hey there. How are you?-C

Good. Thanks. :)-B

They continued to exchange a variety of pleasantries and standard inquiries until they both ran out of them. Carson had waited all morning for that moment and had thought even longer about how she would word it when she managed to ask Bree out for the first time. She had sort of already asked her out, so it was time for the details.

So, I was thinking about heading down to Lake Lure tomorrow. Maybe do Chimney Rock Park? Would you be interested in joining me?-C

I haven't been there in years. I think that would be wonderful. -B

Great! I will pick you up around 8, if that's good for you?-C

That sounds perfect. :) -B

:) I look forward to it very much. See you then.-C

Carson waited. She hoped there would have been another text, but there wasn't. She was disappointed that her last statement had pretty much closed the door for any continued conversation. She smacked her forehead with her phone.

"Not good?" Kelli asked from atop the workbench where she had perched herself.

"What? Oh, no. I mean, yes. Good."

"So why the forehead abuse?"

"Because I just feel like I'm in junior high and just giggled and hung up on my first crush all over again."

"So this is what it looks like when Ms. Carson Harper has a crush? Squeeee. It's adorable."

"Shut up, asshole," Carson said as she felt her face set fire. "I'm going upstairs."

❖

Bree paced around her living room. "Friends. Just friends. Friends go hiking and shopping. Ugh." She flopped herself onto the couch and smooshed her face into a pillow.

She knew there was nothing platonic about how or why Carson had asked her out. The "friends" tactic was a dirty one, and Bree had fallen for it hook, line, and sinker. How could she say no to an offer of friendship? Carson wasn't the jerk she had expected her to be, after all. She slammed the pillow down.

"Who am I kidding? This is SO a date." Bree didn't want it to be a date. There was nowhere their relationship could or would go beyond friends. But in a defiant contradiction to her physical tantrum, Bree couldn't hold back the excitement that built within her when she thought about it. She very much looked forward to spending a day with Carson out in the fresh air. *An intoxicating combination.*

Bree glanced out the window and saw that the kitchen light in the main house was on, which meant that her uncle was finally awake. She needed to spend the rest of her time with an actual person instead of just the voices in her head. She let herself into the kitchen and poured two cups of the coffee from the fresh brewed pot. Jim knew her so well that she was certain he'd made the extra in anticipation of her and her bundled nerves. She set the cups on the table and slid into the chair. She stared down into her mug and watched the coffee and cream swirl into a delicious caramel color.

"Good morning, sweetheart. Did you even put any coffee in that cup?" he asked as he squeezed her shoulder.

"Just whatever dripped off the spoon after I stirred the half pound of sugar into yours." Bree grinned at him.

"Oooh, brat!"

She stuck her tongue out at him as he sat at the table across from her.

"Are you ready for your da—uh, day at the lake?"

"My date?" His eyes bulged out at her, and he clinched his lips together. "Yeah, I know. I said it wasn't a date, but by definition, it is. A date. Let's not make a big deal about it."

"Oh. Okay. So are you ready for your, uh, for today then?" he asked as he looked around the table at her clothing selection. "Is that what you're wearing?"

"What? Seriously?" Bree stood and spun around. "What's wrong with this? Is there something wrong with this?" Bree tugged at her fitted and worn Superman T-shirt. "I have a zippered hoodie thingy that I'm wearing over it. And these are cargo pants. There're made for hiking. And for hauling snacks." She pulled open the pockets and made a show of their expansive transport potential.

"Whoa, kiddo. Calm down. You look fine, great in fact. I meant because you guys are taking her b—" Before he finished his sentence, they were interrupted by a loud rumble outside in the driveway.

Bree's eyes flew open in surprise as she stared at him. "Her what?" Her stomach flopped, and the handful of nervous butterflies she'd had turned into a hundred fluttering ones. "Is that…her? She…we…a motorcycle?" Bree couldn't bring herself to look out the window. She clutched the back of the chair and hoped it would steady her legs. She was getting tired of being knocked off her feet every time Carson came around. The rumble stopped and Bree stared as a shadow appeared through the shaded window of the kitchen door. Her heart pounded in her ears. When she heard the knock, she gasped. "Oh, God."

Her uncle moved toward the door, but before he reached it, Carson let herself in. Bree was frozen and clutched the chair with such a tight grip she thought the back would snap in her hands. Carson's helmet was tucked beneath her arm when she entered, and Bree's breath caught in her throat. When she tousled her hair with a rough hand, Bree thought her knees would give out.

"Hey, old man," Carson said to Jim as she set her helmet on the counter and grabbed a cup from the cabinet above the coffee maker. Bree couldn't help but notice how at ease she was in her uncle's home. She moved with purpose and smooth confidence. As Carson poured her coffee, Bree just stared. She wore a slim pair of the world's luckiest Levi's, a cobalt blue T-shirt, and a black leather jacket that looked like it was made just for her. "Damn." Bree gasped as soon as she realized she had spoken aloud. She prayed it was the gasp and not the exclamation that caused Carson to look over at her. The look on Carson's face made Bree's insides melt. She felt a flush of heat start in her belly and spread fast and low between her legs. Carson flashed a cocky grin that said she knew exactly what she'd done to Bree.

"Hey."

"Hey...hi." Bree giggled and twirled her hair. Carson laughed. Bree was surprised at just how sexy her laugh was, even though it was clearly directed at her. "Oh geez. I just did that, didn't I?" Bree felt her cheeks turn red and buried her face in her hands. For an instant, she wished she were invisible until she felt the two strong hands on her wrists that pulled her hands down between them. Bree looked up into Carson's eyes and held her breath.

"It's okay. I thought it was cute," Carson said as she maintained her grip on Bree's hands.

Bree could've stood that way forever if Carson had promised never to look away. Against her will, Bree's attention was drawn to her uncle, who clanked his spoon in his mug. It was his obvious attempt to break both the awkward silence and sizzling energy that had filled the room. It worked. Bree pried her hands from Carson's grip. The result was an instant sting of loss. She hadn't noticed, but she must have shivered because Carson suggested a heavier jacket for the ride.

Bree looked down at her arms and the goose bumps that rose on her skin. "Oh, okay. Good idea. I have a leather one next door. I'll go get it and be right back." Bree excused herself and made a quick turn toward her house. It took everything she had to keep her pace slow and calm. The last thing she needed was to trip and fall on her face in the yard.

While she was in her closet, she took the opportunity to change out of her cargos into a pair of jeans. "Friends. Just friends," Bree chanted as she slipped into her black and red leather jacket and pulled her hair back into a neat ponytail. She wouldn't be able to hike the trails in leather, so she folded her hoodie around her arm and headed back down to the main house.

Jim and Carson waited outside next to the bike, a gorgeous black custom cruiser. Bree didn't know a thing about motorcycles except that they were sexy as hell, and a gorgeous woman on one was twice that. Bree guaranteed that her uncle was reviewing his mental safety checklist before he allowed Bree to leave on Carson's motorcycle.

As Bree watched Jim and Carson chat next to the bike, Bree thought about Marion. She pondered how she would have looked in a black leather jacket. She didn't know because that wasn't something Marion would have ever worn even though she knew Bree's penchant for the sexy biker look. Marion had a significant fear of motorcycles for herself and for those around her. It was a protective concern that Bree had loved about her, even if it kept her from doing something she enjoyed.

It was always at the most inopportune moments that Marion popped into Bree's mind. The smallest things always brought back various thoughts of her and their life together. She wondered if an entire day would ever pass where she didn't think of Marion at least once. Thankfully, the memories of Marion were blown away once Carson's eyes met hers. Bree was excited and couldn't wait to feel what it was like to pull herself tight against Carson and wrap her arms around her. She wondered how well they would *fit*.

"That jacket…wow. It's, uh, it looks good on you," Carson said.

"Thanks. I'm excited that I get to use it for its intended purpose, and not just because it's smokin' hot." Bree blushed and laughed at her own wit.

"Oh, it's definitely that. Are you ready?"

"I am."

❖

Carson didn't know what she expected when she had arrived to pick up Bree, but she'd been pleasantly surprised and aroused when she saw Bree in the kitchen. She didn't think it was possible for Bree to be more beautiful than she was in that moment. That was until Carson watched Bree come from across the yard in fitted denim jeans and a sexy as hell red and black leather jacket. Carson felt herself burn with desire at the thought of Bree's soft full breasts pushed against her back.

The bike may have been the best idea Carson had ever had, and from the look on Bree's face, she thought so as well. *Point one for me.*

Carson grabbed the extra helmet that sat on the seat and handed it to Bree. Bree slipped on the helmet as Jim watched like a nervous mother hen. Carson checked the fit and tightened the strap under Bree's chin. "Looks good," she said to both Bree and Jim. Carson slipped her leg over the bike and kicked it to life. Once she was settled, she motioned for Bree to get on.

Carson felt a sharp jolt of electricity surge through her when Bree slipped onto the seat and wrapped her legs around Carson's hips. She began to think that having Bree so intimately pressed against her for the forty-minute ride wasn't such a wise idea after all. When Bree slipped her arms around Carson's waist and pulled her close, Carson closed her eyes. She reveled in the perfect feel of Bree's body on hers. Carson thought that even if Bree changed her mind that second she'd have been blessed for those few flawless moments. She was thankful that Bree didn't change her mind, and at that moment the day had become the best one Carson ever remembered having.

Carson was delighted by how Bree's body moved in sync with hers as they rode along the winding roads and switchbacks of the beautiful North Carolina mountains. She enjoyed the ride so much that she found herself disappointed once they reached Chimney Rock Village. She drove the remaining two miles into the park well under the speed limit and savored the last moments of their intimate connection.

When they parked and Bree slid off the bike, Carson felt the cool air touch her back. She felt the shiver of the loss of Bree's warmth inside and out. She almost made up an excuse to get Bree back on the bike, but she didn't. They would always have the ride back home, and Carson looked forward to walking and talking with Bree. She was excited to enjoy the beauty of the park and Bree.

They browsed the map and picked the Skyline Trail. It was a moderate hike that hit many of the park's popular sites including the beautiful pool formation at the top of the falls. Carson stowed their jackets and helmets before they headed toward their adventure. They strolled into the dim cave that led to the fastest and easiest way up the twenty-six stories of solid mountain rock—an elevator. While Carson wasn't fond of the potential for being trapped in a steel box 250 feet underground, she preferred the easy thirty-five-second ride versus the twenty-five-minute thigh-torturing trek.

CHAPTER THIRTEEN

Carson's uneasiness was palpable as they waited at the end of the cool tunnel with the dozen other guests who crowded together. From what Bree could remember from her childhood, the elevator operator would attempt to pack the entire group into the metal box like sardines. Bree watched Carson as she nervously surveyed the people around them. She had an overwhelming need to comfort Carson. "You know, we don't have to take the elevator." Bree stroked Carson's forearm.

Carson glanced down at the hand on her arm and placed her own on top of it. "It's okay. It's faster this way." She smiled at Bree and rubbed her thumb over Bree's wrist.

"If you're sure," Bree said as she smiled back. She made no attempt to take her hand back. "It's quite cool in here, isn't it?" Bree used it as an excuse to move in closer to Carson. She closed her eyes as her other senses went into overdrive. She was intoxicated by the subtle scent of Carson's cologne.

"It feels perfect to me."

When the elevator arrived, the doors opened and the crowd pushed their way inside. They waited until everyone else had boarded before the operator motioned for them to enter. "Last on, first off." Bree winked up at Carson. As the door closed them in, Bree pulled Carson in tighter. She wanted Carson to know she was there if she needed her. At least, that's what she told herself.

The thirty-second ride seemed more like three seconds because when the doors opened, Bree wasn't ready to let go. She looked up at Carson, gave a little squeeze, and smiled. "That wasn't so bad, huh?"

"Wanna go again?" Carson joked.

The thought of saying yes flittered through her mind when someone behind them cleared their throat. "Maybe later." Bree laughed as she let go of Carson's arm and exited the elevator. They moved just fast enough to avoid being trampled by the other riders.

"That was a close one," Carson said. "I'm going to get some water. Would you like anything?"

"Water would be great, thanks." Bree watched Carson as she walked toward the counter. She pretended to look at a rack of overpriced sunglasses as she raked her eyes brazenly over Carson's body. Never had she wanted to be a pair of Levi's more in her life. She spun the rack and stared unfocused as it whirled around. Bree imagined herself reaching around and slipping her hands into Carson's tight back pockets. She fantasized about how she would squeeze and pull Carson into her. She closed her eyes and let herself enjoy the vision her mind created.

"Did you want sunglasses?"

"What?" Startled from her fantasy, Bree flung her arms up and knocked several pairs of sunglasses from the rack as it revolved. She managed to make the situation worse as she continued to flail around in an attempt to catch the items but managed to do nothing more than swat them to the ground. "Oh, for fuck's sake. Seriously?" Fed up, Bree put her arms to her sides and let the remaining shades fall where they might.

She looked over at Carson, who was straining to maintain her decorum and not burst into hysterical tears and laughter.

"Are you okay?" Carson asked.

"I'm fine," Bree murmured as she knelt to pick up the glasses off the floor. She felt her face glow crimson, and there was a moment where she contemplated the option to stay crouched on the floor for the rest of the day. When a hand was offered down to her she hesitated, but Bree knew she couldn't find a sane excuse to stay there, no matter how embarrassed she was. Bree took Carson's hand and stood. Carson took the few pairs of glasses Bree held and placed them back on the rack. She then slipped her hand under Bree's chin and raised her head until their eyes met.

"Hey. Sorry I startled you."

"It's okay. As you've figured out, I'm kind of a...well, I'm a hot mess."

"Yeah, I noticed. But I kind of like it." Carson smiled. "But for today, let me walk on the cliff side, okay?"

"Hey." Bree swatted at Carson. "Yeah, that's probably a good idea."

They wandered outside and paused on the patio for a quick minute. Bree took out her phone and snapped a picture of the large Chimney Rock monolith—the park's namesake. It was an impressive sight, no matter how many times she'd seen it when she was younger. The cloud-capped mountains in the distance added another level of serenity to the moment, and Bree welcomed the peaceful contentment. When Carson wandered into the frame, Bree's spirit beamed. She insisted that Carson turn around to pose for a proper photograph.

Carson's apparent definition of "proper" was exaggerated model poses, but that did little to stop Bree as she snapped dozens of images in succession. As Bree put her phone back into her pocket a woman tapped her on the shoulder. "Would you like me to get one of both of you together?"

Bree hesitated long enough for Carson to answer for her. "Yes, please." Carson trotted over and thanked the woman before she handed over her phone as well. "Can you get one on mine, too?"

Bree felt her hand being pulled as Carson dragged her back toward the railing. When they stopped, Carson spun Bree around, wrapped her arms around her waist, and pulled her back against her firm body. Bree felt her stomach flutter at the feeling of being embraced in such an assertive manner, so confident and comfortable. They stood together long enough to allow the woman to take a couple of pictures on each phone. Bree hesitated for a second before she stepped out of Carson's arms and took back the phones. They thanked her before they both flipped through their galleries to see the images. Bree was more than pleasantly surprised by how they looked together.

"Should we get started?" Carson asked.

Bree couldn't help but smile. "Yes." So far, everything was beyond her expectations and she was excited for what the rest of the day held. If she could keep from falling over herself or over Carson, everything would be great. Although, she knew at that point it was too late for both.

❖

Carson and Bree stopped at the bottom of a massive scaffold staircase. Carson always managed to forget just how many steps it was to get up the cliff to the rest of the trail. She had no doubt that her legs were going to remind her for many days afterward. For the most part the trip up was easy, because she made Bree go first. The reason was twofold. One was because she knew the trek would be far more enjoyable if she got to watch Bree ascend ahead of her. And two was because Bree was accident-prone and Carson wasn't kidding when she claimed the outside lane as a precaution. They both made it, albeit winded, to the top without incident. "So far so good," Carson announced.

"Keep it up, smarty," Bree said without turning back and Carson laughed.

They started up the path. They paused to read the large sign and map posted at the trailhead. A few seasoned hikers, there for their daily workout regimen, breezed past them. Carson was fine with that since she didn't imagine either of them were interested in making the day about racing or exercising.

They walked along the trail and pointed out random sights along the way. It was evident that Bree loved to take pictures. They stopped often so she could snap images of lichen covered tree stumps or the intricate detail of the exposed marbled boulders. On more than one occasion Carson found herself the focal point of Bree's photography, although she pretended to be unaware each time she noticed. Carson couldn't take her eyes off Bree long enough to be bothered with a camera. Instead she practiced her ability to memorize every dip and curve of Bree from head to toe, and so far, it had worked beautifully.

Carson was a little surprised when they came to the end of the Skyline Trail where the stairs led down to the top of the falls. She had always remembered it taking much longer to accomplish. It was her favorite place in the entire park. During the heat of spring and summer, it was a popular gathering place for locals. The ice-cold cascade of fresh water filled in the staggered pools before it spilled over and dropped four hundred feet down the cliff face on its journey to the Broad River. In the warmer seasons, children and adults would wade into the frigid water to cool off, whereas Carson preferred to perch herself upon a dry boulder. She liked to listen to the sounds of the water as it flowed from Fall Creek and tumbled over a series of drops down the hillside. She could always find her peace that way. No matter how many other people ambled around her, it made her feel free. On that day it seemed that Carson had been given the luckiest of breaks, as it was just her and Bree all alone to enjoy the sights and sounds.

Carson climbed onto her chosen slab of rock and held her hand out to Bree. Once they were both safely aloft, Carson lay down on her back and invited Bree to join her. Bree hesitated just a second before she positioned herself against Carson's side. For the first time since she had held Bree against her earlier that day, Carson felt complete. She was amazed at how whole her entire body and mind felt when Bree touched her. It was then that she realized just how partial she had felt all the other times. No one had ever made her feel emptier or more fulfilled with a single touch. They stared into the canopy of trees above them and listened as the water rushed past. With Bree at her side, it had become Carson's new happy place.

"This is pretty awesome, isn't it?" Carson asked with her eyes closed.

"Perfect," Bree answered in a whisper. Bree shifted her body and pulled her camera phone from her pocket. As she held it above them, she tilted her head closer to Carson and rested her chin on Carson's shoulder. Bree snapped a few pictures and then slid the phone back into her pocket without moving her head from where it was.

Carson's body felt warm and perfect where Bree's body connected with it, yet the rock they were lying on had begun to send a chill through her. "This rock is like an ice cube. I don't think I can feel my ass cheeks any more. But I don't want to move."

Bree laughed and sat up. As she got to her feet, she held out her hand to Carson. "Well, we can't have you getting frostbite on your bum, now can we?" Bree laughed.

Carson jumped down off the rock and held up her arms for Bree. Bree looked around, leery about Carson's ability to pull off what she asked for. Carson had no doubts. "Just come here."

Bree reached out for Carson, who swooped her off the rock with a suave grace. Bree squealed and giggled as Carson swung her around and then lowered her down onto the solid ground. Carson didn't let go. She continued to hold Bree at the waist and refused to let even light penetrate the space between them. Bree grinned. "I must admit, I had my doubts about you pulling that off."

"And why is that?" Carson squeezed Bree's waist just a hint and raised an eyebrow as she waited for the answer.

"Honestly? I just knew I was going to slip or trip and take us both down in flames."

They laughed until Carson slipped one arm around Bree's entire waist and pulled her hard against her chest. Carson watched as Bree licked her lips and she needed to taste the sweet tongue that slid over them. Carson felt almost combustible. She brushed away a stray curl that had blown across Bree's face and her eyes fluttered shut. Bree raised her chin to offer her lips to Carson. "Fire is dangerous," Carson whispered against Bree's mouth.

Bree's eyes flickered open and she stared into the depths of Carson's as they darkened with desire. "But it's also so beautiful." Her voice was breathless as she closed her own eyes and lowered her lips to Bree's. The perfect silence and heat of the moment was pierced by the screams and laughter of what Carson decided was a passel of devil spawn.

As if doused with a bucket of ice water, they jumped apart.

They both watched as a group of children and their chaperones trampled like a herd of elephants down the stairs toward them. Carson looked back at Bree, who did not attempt to hide the look of utter disappointment on her face. It was one that was certain to match Carson's own. "Well, I guess that's that."

"It would seem so."

"We should probably start heading back down anyway. We can get some lunch, either in the lounge here or down in the village. It's up to you."

Bree chose one of the many restaurants down in the village. As they headed down the Cliffside trail, Bree mentioned her parents for the first time. She told Carson a story about how her father had brought her to the park when she was very young. Of course Carson knew that they'd died in a traffic accident, along with Jim's wife, when Bree was eight years old. By choice, Carson had a nonexistent relationship with her own parents, but it saddened her to know that Bree was never afforded the opportunity to know her own.

"I remember my father climbing those rocks," she said as she pointed up into the hillside. "I think he was attempting to re-create a scene from the movie *The Last of the Mohicans*. My mother was beside herself, calling him names, and demanding that he 'get down this instant.' On his way down, he slipped and landed on his butt in a mud puddle. My mother was so furious at first, but when my father and I couldn't stop laughing she eventually gave up and joined in."

Carson adored the way Bree's face lit up as she told the story. It hadn't been long after that day that she had lost them. "That sounds like a wonderful memory." Carson reached out for Bree's hand, and their fingers curled together. Their hands remained clasped for the rest of the hike down the mountain. They separated just long enough to squeeze through the narrow passage of Wild Cat Trap.

Bree and Carson enjoyed their lunch on an open-air patio that overlooked the Broad River and the Rocky Broad Riverwalk. They sat and talked about work and school and their combined love of all things Biltmore. She could've sat and talked with her all day or been just as content to sit in silence in her presence. It didn't matter to Carson in the least, and that was a very new feeling for her. She couldn't recall a single person she had ever wanted to do nothing at all with, not even Kelli.

As with the ride in, Carson was overjoyed by the feeling of Bree holding tight behind her as they rode home. She couldn't help but notice how Bree held her a little tighter and a little closer than before, and Carson's entire body took pleasure in it. They pulled into Bree's driveway as the sun had begun to set. The temperature had dropped, yet every part of Carson was a smoldering flame. She helped Bree off the bike with one arm, then took the helmet from her and without looking hooked it on the handlebars. She didn't want to take her eyes off Bree for a moment longer than she had to. Carson was mesmerized by the light of the setting sun and the soft glow it had cast over Bree's face. She had never before been so captivated by one woman.

"I should go let Jim know I'm home."

"Of course. Let me walk you up." Carson grabbed Bree's hand and led her to the kitchen door. As they stood on the steps, Carson took Bree's hands in hers and pulled her in until their bodies pressed together. "That was the best day I've had in, well, ever I think."

"It was wonderful."

"It really was." Carson's heart melted when Bree looked into her eyes and gave a sweet smile. She was so beautiful, and Carson thought if she didn't kiss her she might burst at the seams. She lowered her head as Bree closed her eyes.

Suddenly, the kitchen door opened. "Hey. How was… uh…" Jim stuttered.

If looks could kill, Jim would have been dead in the doorway from the daggers both Carson and Bree shot at him. "No. No way," Carson said as she reached over, grabbed the knob, and pulled. "Go away." Jim looked shocked but jumped back as the door closed in front of him.

Bree chuckled but was silenced as Carson cupped her face with her hands and kissed her. Carson had waited all day for the chance to kiss Bree. So soft and sweet, she struggled to maintain her fervor. When she felt the warmth of Bree's tongue slide against her lip, she lost the battle. It was the trigger she knew would release her fierce desire for Bree. Carson slid her hands down Bree's back and pulled her close. She could feel the soft fullness of Bree's breasts as they pressed into her. Bree parted her lips and allowed Carson's tongue to dance in her mouth. When she heard Bree's soft muffled moan of pleasure, Carson felt a rush of heat between her legs.

Carson could have spent the entire night kissing and caressing Bree, but the thought of an anxious Jim pacing behind the closed door threw her off her game. "Do you think we should let him out now?"

Bree laughed. "I guess if we must."

Carson opened the door and revealed a stern-faced, cross-armed Jim who tapped his parental foot. "Two more minutes and I was going to start flashing porch lights."

CHAPTER FOURTEEN

Jim was adamant on Monday morning that he and Bree ride into work together. It wasn't an out of the blue request because they almost always carpooled, but Bree knew the real reason for his insistence. After Carson had dropped her off and said her good-byes to Jim, Bree hadn't stuck around for his interrogation. She remembered his tactics from high school where he gave her the third degree every time she came home from a date. Bree imagined that his brain was in hyperdrive about her and Carson.

It wasn't that she tried to avoid the discussion. It was just that she wanted to enjoy the moments to herself for a while longer. They were slipping away with each second that passed, and she didn't want to put too much thought into it. Plus, Bree had no idea how she could have even begun to describe what she had felt in every minute since Carson had kissed her. A brew of emotions churned in her head, but one overpowered all the rest: guilt. Each thought of Carson was consumed by one of Marion, as if her memory and Marion's were fighting for their rightful place within Bree's mind.

As Carson held her and brushed her lips over her, she felt for the first time as if healing was within her grasp. She thought for that brief moment that she was on her way to being happy once again. It had been so long since she'd kissed anyone other than Marion. She had vowed never to love or make love to another woman for the rest of her life. She had given her entire body and soul to her, and she had never asked for it back. Bree didn't have the right to give those things to someone else, even if it was just a simple kiss. But she had, and deep inside she knew she would have done it again.

❖

As soon as Bree had moved back, she and Jim fell back into their routine of Sunday family days. They spent them doing what Jim liked, which was either tinkering around the house or sauntering around town. In the evening, one or the other would make dinner as they bantered about which movie to watch. It was their thing, and Bree adored it. Yet, for the first time Bree chose to plant herself on her couch and text with Carson all day long. Bree didn't think there was a single thing they hadn't talked about. Although she steered clear of any discussion that involved sex and exes. She wanted to avoid throwing gas on the smoldering fire inside her, but she didn't want to throw ice water on it either. They both seemed content to keep their conversation within the realm of flirty, getting to know you chitchat. Carson was a master at seduction, and she never failed to say all the right things to rouse Bree's lusts.

Jim drove and Bree scrolled through the texts from the day before. She knew she smiled like a fool, but she couldn't help it. Carson had a way with words and Bree couldn't remember the last time someone had made her feel so special and beautiful.

Bree looked at the picture she had selected for Carson's contact image. She had taken it, along with many others, during their trip to Chimney Rock. She flipped from her texts to her gallery and browsed the pictures for the umpteenth time. She couldn't help herself. There wasn't a single picture of Carson that wasn't stunning. She pinched at the screen and enlarged one of the images and zoomed in on Carson's soft pink lips. Bree wanted to feel those warm lips on hers again soon. When her phone beeped and vibrated in her hand, she let out a startled squeak. The squeak was followed by a giggle when she realized that it was a text from Carson.

Good morning, my alluring sweetheart-C

She had been called beautiful before. Marion had said it on occasion, usually after they'd fought. It was when Carson called her alluring that Bree felt a rush of bliss flow through her. No one had ever called her alluring, and it was possibly the most romantic and arousing word she had ever heard.

Bree struggled to find the perfect response when Jim interrupted her blushing girlish brain paralysis. "I'll only ask you one thing about it."

Still smiling from ear to ear, Bree turned to him. "Huh? Hi. What?" He repeated himself. "I was wondering how long it would take." She looked again at her phone and then lowered it to her lap. "Fine, but you only get one, so you better make it good."

"Well, what if your answer requires additional questions for clarification?"

"Well, then I suggest you choose a yes or no question just to be safe." Bree laughed.

"Ugh, okay. Then I would like to reserve the right to hold my question until another time."

"Hmm. I have a feeling this will come back to bite me in the ass somehow, but since I don't have much to say about things at this moment, I think that's fine." Bree wasn't ready to answer any questions, even a simple yes or no one.

Bree looked out the window and then at the time on the

dash. She thought if they went any slower they'd have been traveling in reverse. If her uncle stepped on it, they could get to work in time for her to see Carson before she had to start her first scheduled tour. Bree hoped for more than two seconds with her, but if time allowed for a quick smile and hello, it would be more than enough to start her day. When they pulled into the parking lot, Bree jumped out and bolted for the building. "Six minutes." Bree sent a text without slowing down.

Hey you. Good morning :) Are you in yet?-B

So much for the witty and flirty response she had wanted to send. When she got to Carson's office, her heart sank. It appeared that Carson hadn't even made it into the office or at least to her desk yet. Bree looked around and then checked the time on her phone. "Dammit." How did it take her five minutes to get from the parking lot to the office? Disappointed, she left the office and dashed toward the tour muster station.

As usual, there was a healthy group of anxious guests who mulled about as they waited for her. Bree approached the group, announced herself, and welcomed everyone to the Biltmore. The group circled around her and listened as she reviewed the rules and tour expectations. All of a sudden, everyone's attention was drawn to the sight and sound of someone running toward them. The group parted to allow Carson through. She slid to a halt in front of Bree and pulled a beautiful bouquet of lilies from behind her back. Bree's face flushed, and her mouth dropped open in surprise.

"What are you doing?" Bree whispered to Carson and looked around as everyone stared at them.

"Just saying good morning." Carson looked amused.

"You're crazy. Do you know that?" Bree looked down at the pink and white stargazer lilies. She didn't even remember when she'd told Carson that they were her favorite flower.

"I am crazy," Carson said before she leaned in to Bree's ear and whispered, "for you. Have a great day." As Carson turned to leave, she addressed the guests. "Enjoy your tour, ladies and gentlemen. This is Biltmore's best and most knowledgeable guide, and her beauty is a definite bonus."

Once Carson was gone, the group turned their attention back to Bree, who still stood in awe and clutched the bunch against her chest with one hand. With her free hand she had a death grip on the railing in order to keep herself in an upright position. She blushed as everyone stared at her and she stared down the hall toward where Carson had disappeared.

Bree snapped out of her daze and smiled back at them. "Well, okay, shall we be on our way?"

❖

Carson walked away from the group with more confidence than she felt. She had every intention of meeting Bree in the parking lot that morning to give her the flowers. Her truck had refused to start, and she had to take her bike, but Carson refused to let it ruin her plan to surprise Bree. Somehow she managed to stuff the bouquet into her jacket without damaging a single bloom in the bunch, although she'd succeeded in pollinating her shirt with a layer of yellow dust.

Once Carson made it around the corner and out of sight of a very overwhelmed Bree and an astonished group of guests, she stopped to catch her breath. Carson felt like she hadn't taken a single breath since she had amped herself up and made her gallant move. Her heart raced, and she thought it would pound right out of her chest. Carson couldn't believe how much the simple thought of Bree affected her, let alone the sight, scent, or heaven help her, taste of her. Carson thought Bree smelled beautiful, like a soft mixture of citrus and sunshine, and she tasted even better. Her pulse returned to a semi-normal state, and Carson allowed herself to peek back around the corner at Bree, who led her group up the staircase. Before Carson pulled her gaze away, her heart fluttered when she watched Bree bring the bouquet up to steal another smell.

For a split second, anxiety rushed through Carson after an unexpected sense of loss filled her chest as she watched Bree disappear up the stairs. Against the irrational need she felt to wait for her to return, Carson headed toward her office and checked the time on her phone. She saw the text from Bree and couldn't help but smile. She was in the midst of her reply when she felt a hand grip her shoulder. "Oh no. Not you, too?"

"What? Huh?" Still smiling, Carson looked up at Jim.

"I just spent twenty minutes driving in with a grinning, giggling teenager. And now I see that it's contagious."

"I'm not giggling. I don't giggle. This is not giggling." Carson tried and failed to keep a straight face as she defended herself. She gave up. She didn't care if someone saw her smiling or even giggling; she was happy. "Okay, maybe I giggle sometimes." She still attempted to say it in a controlled manner.

"Well, contagious or not, I'm overjoyed that both of my girls are happy and smiling." Jim put his arm around Carson's shoulders and pulled her into his side. "It makes me happy. But you both need to be careful. Just take it slow."

They walked that way until they got to the door to Carson's workspace. Jim excused himself for a meeting, and Carson went in to get started for the day. She sat at her desk and took out her phone to finish the text she had started earlier. She knew that Bree's first tour was an hour and a half, and she would have a thirty-minute break before her next one began.

Hey you. Can you meet me in my office on your next break?-C

Yes. I'll see you soon.-B

After an hour and a half had passed, Carson's heart began to pound before she even looked at the time. She just knew that Bree was on her way. She wiped her palms on her pant legs as she swiveled back and forth on her tall drafting stool. Carson heard the door handle turn, and she inhaled deeply. When she saw Bree she forgot how to exhale. She held her breath for fear that if she moved a single muscle Bree would stop, or worse, disappear altogether. Bree didn't disappear, and she stopped when her hips touched Carson's knees. Carson knew if she didn't breathe soon she would pass out, but as Bree's hips pressed between her thighs, she wasn't sure she hadn't already died and gone to heaven. She had never before needed anyone or anything with such desperation.

When Bree spoke the world began to spin again. "Hi," she said.

Carson took a breath and inhaled the delicious scent that was Bree. "Hi," was the only word Carson managed to say.

Bree giggled and Carson's heart skipped. When Bree placed her hand on Carson's thigh and squeezed ever so gently, Carson could no longer control herself. She jumped off the chair and it slammed into the desk behind her. The swift movement and noise startled Bree backward. Carson was unfazed as she grabbed Bree's arms and wrapped them behind her neck. Carson gripped Bree's waist and pushed her back toward the door she had just entered through. When Bree was pressed against the door, Carson kissed her. She claimed her lips with heated enthusiasm. All day, Carson had thought of nothing but the need to taste Bree.

Bree opened her mouth and offered herself to Carson. Bree moaned in pleasure and arched herself into Carson's body. Carson slipped her leg between Bree's and ran her hands down to the small of her back. She pulled her in quick and hard against her strong thigh. Carson felt Bree's heat on her leg, and it drove her mad with need. She needed to feel Bree in her hand.

Carson's body was ablaze and her center was molten. She knew that Bree was just as hot and ready as she was. She brought her hand around and slipped it between her legs along the seam of Bree's pants. She rubbed the fabric, and Bree whimpered the moment Carson found the perfect spot. She kissed Bree's neck and nibbled at her ear. "You are so beautiful, and I want you so bad." With one hand, she unbuttoned Bree's slacks and began to slip her hand inside the waistband. The tip of her fingers skimmed over the silky fabric of Bree's panties. Carson cupped her hand around the pulsing middle and pressed a finger against the swollen peak. Bree was wet and ready to be pleased, and she cried out with desire.

As Carson slipped her hand between the lace panties and smooth skin, Bree stopped her. Carson looked down and saw Bree's hand that held Carson's wrist. She looked up, concerned that she had pushed Bree too far. "Are you okay?" she asked as she pulled back her hand.

Bree placed her hand on Carson's face. "I'm fine. And while I want nothing more than to fulfill this fantasy, I just don't think this is how I want it to be…the first time. I think I need to slow down."

"Of course, sweetheart, whatever you want." Carson offered to help Bree reassemble her clothing but gave up and let Bree do it on her own. She brushed a strand of Bree's hair back in place.

"Are you mad?" Bree asked.

"What? Oh my God. No, I'm not mad." Carson rubbed Bree's shoulders. "I would never be mad at you for stopping yourself from doing something you weren't ready for." Carson cupped Bree's face in her hand and brushed a thumb along her lips. "Never." Carson was taken aback that Bree would think for a moment that she would be upset or angry that Bree had stopped them from doing something she wasn't ready for. While it was a new experience for her in particular, she could never have imagined being enraged by it.

"Okay." Bree smiled as Carson leaned in and kissed her sweetly. "Mmm, I do love doing that, though. Maybe you can come by tonight for dinner and a movie with my uncle and me? Popcorn and cuddling, maybe some more kissing?"

"Anything. Well, cuddling maybe, but I am not kissing your uncle," Carson said. They both shivered at the uncomfortable thought and laughed.

Chapter Fifteen

Carson lingered in the lobby as she had done every day for a week. As work picked up with the third-floor project, she didn't get to see Bree as much as she wanted to. As that was all the time, anything less than that was insufficient. She had never before had such an insatiable desire to be with another person. Not even the memories of their brief and heated encounters in Carson's office were enough to curb her longing. If anything, it made them stronger. Carson couldn't remember having waited so long to get what she wanted. Her growing need to have Bree in every countless way was as exciting as it was unsettling.

Carson saw Bree and Jim as soon as they entered the building. Sometimes Carson thought she could feel Bree long before she ever saw her. A smile lit up Bree's face as soon as they spotted each other, and Carson's heart leapt. She was like the rising sun, and Carson didn't know how she'd ever begun a day without it.

Every morning, Carson forced herself to stand in the same spot and resist any urge she had to sprint across the foyer and scoop the beautiful Bree into her arms. It had become her daily lesson in willpower and perseverance. However, once Bree was within reach Carson didn't hesitate to act on her impulses and pull her into a tight, wanton embrace. She kissed Bree for as long as she could before the sound of Jim clearing his throat ruined the mood. As always, Carson huffed and released Bree. She sneered at Jim as if he had just confiscated her favorite toy. "Good morning, Jim. You know, you're taking this protective dad thing overboard, don't you think?"

"Overboard? Nah. I haven't even shown you my shotgun collection yet," Jim said with a wink.

"Oh, good grief. You're both so full of shit. I have to go. Can the two of you play nice today or do I need to get Barbara to watch you?" Bree asked as she pointed back and forth between Carson and Jim.

"We'll be fine, dear," Jim said as Bree kissed first him and then Carson on the cheek before she walked away.

Carson watched her leave. As soon as Bree was out of earshot, Carson turned to Jim. Even then, she spoke softly. "So, Bree's birthday is on Saturday and I was wondering if you had anything planned?"

"Um, not exactly. It's been a while since she's been home for a birthday, but when she was it was just a low-key dinner. Why? Do you?"

"Not so much. I was thinking a surprise dinner at the Grand Boho with a few of us?"

"That sounds like a fantastic idea, Car. I think she'll love it."

"Perfect. I'll get it worked out and then give you the details. Sweet." Carson popped Jim in the arm before she skipped off into the office area.

❖

Carson pulled her truck into Bree and Jim's driveway. She got out of the truck and spotted Jim who peeked through the miniblinds of the kitchen door. It was his poor, albeit humorous, attempt not to be seen. Carson used her hand and smoothed away the smile in case Bree also watched from her kitchen window. She rolled her eyes at Jim and trotted up the hill toward Bree's front door. Carson didn't know why she was so nervous. They'd been on a single date before. Still, it felt as though they were about to have their first real one. She took a deep breath and rang the bell.

Carson couldn't have imagined how dazzling Bree would look the moment she opened the door. Carson stumbled backward off the stoop as all the air rushed from her lungs. Bree stood in the door with a sparkling smile and the richest eyes Carson had ever seen. Her hair was swept back loose and sexy to expose a long, luscious neck. Carson couldn't help it as her eyes traced the sinuous lines of Bree's skin down to her dangerously bare chest. The deep V of Bree's crimson gown was cut low between her ample breasts. Lucky for them both that Carson was paralyzed in awe or she'd have swept Bree into her arms and taken her on the floor of the foyer.

"Bree Whitley…you look…You are so beautiful," Carson managed to say.

Bree raised a seductive eyebrow. "Thank you for noticing, Ms. Harper."

Carson drew Bree in to her. She lowered her head and pleaded, "May I please kiss you?"

Before Bree could answer, their mouths were connected. What had begun tentatively grew into a fevered hunger. Against every desire in her mind and body, Carson pulled away. "Damn, you are amazing. But we should get going if we want to make our reservations."

Carson led Bree down the sidewalk to her truck. She opened the door and helped Bree into the vehicle. When the skirt of her long dress slipped upward, Carson's fingers brushed along the smooth skin of Bree's bare leg. Her mind flashed with arousing images of those legs wrapped around her body. Before she acted on her impulses right in the driveway, she closed the door and walked around the back of the truck to the driver's side. Although she couldn't see him, she knew Jim was on the other side of the door. She winked her signal to proceed with the next phase of the plan.

Carson hadn't told Bree where they were going for dinner so any route she took wouldn't cause suspicion. She had plenty of time before they needed to be at the restaurant, but if Carson was going to make it to their first stop before sunset, she had to get moving. Carson struggled to keep her eyes on the road and not on Bree.

"That dress is amazing. You are amazing." Carson took Bree's hand in hers.

"Thank you. You don't look so bad yourself."

Carson could feel Bree's eyes on her as she drove. "If you keep looking at me like that I'm going to pull this truck over and we'll never make it where we need to be tonight."

Bree pulled Carson's hand into her lap and stroked her forearm with her free hand. "Oh, really?"

Carson emitted a low growl and squeezed Bree's hand. "Really."

Carson pulled the truck over onto the side of the road and Bree's eyes widened. Bree looked around outside and then at Carson. "What are you doing? Where are we?"

Carson smiled and leaned in toward Bree. "I told you I'd pull over if you didn't stop looking at me like that."

Bree smiled as she ran her finger down the bridge of Carson's nose and over her parted lips. She leaned in and brought her lips to where her finger brushed Carson's mouth. "I'm sorry."

Carson could feel the heat of Bree's breath so close. "You don't ever need to be sorry for how you make me feel."

"Good to know." Bree pressed her lips to Carson's. The kiss was full of heat and passion. Neither of them wasted time with light caresses as their tongues tangled together with desperate need. Bree's arms wrapped around Carson's neck and pulled her deeper into her.

Carson moaned with pleasure and raw desire. She wanted to be inside every part of Bree. Carson ran her hand down the length of Bree's long leg until she reached the hem of her dress. She clutched the fabric in her hand and pulled it up over Bree's knee to expose the smooth skin of her thigh. The sound of Bree's wanton whimper sent a rush of heat between Carson's legs. The sound of a vehicle that passed roused her from the trance Bree had her in. Carson looked around and realized if they didn't stop they would miss the real reason she had pulled over. "Shit, we're going to miss it." Carson released Bree and jumped out of the truck.

Confused, Bree watched as Carson rounded the front of the truck to the passenger's side and opened her door. Carson helped her from the truck and led her to a clearing beyond the trees that lined the edge of the roadside parking area. Beyond the small clearing, the steep ground sloped down toward the city. For the first time, Bree realized they were on the mountain that overlooked downtown.

The city skyline was capped by the majestic Blue Ridge Mountains in the distance. As the sun set over the range, it replaced the crystal blue backdrop with clouds that radiated dramatic shades of pink and orange. Bree stood in awe as she watched the sky transform before her eyes, and the lights of the city flickered to life. She could feel the warmth of the sky and the glowing clouds envelop her just as Carson's arms slipped around her waist and pulled Bree back against her. "Happy birthday, Bree Whitley."

Bree could have stayed on the hillside forever with Carson

wrapped around her. She felt safe and secure and would have believed anything in the world was possible in that moment. In those few beautiful minutes, Bree felt the weight of loneliness she'd carried for so long begin to slip away. She felt a hope spark to life deep inside her, and she couldn't have thought of a more perfect or romantic way to have spent her birthday, or any day. When Carson started to release her, she grunted with discontentment. She may have even whined had her stomach not growled when Carson mentioned that their next stop involved food.

"Are you ready?" Carson asked as Bree spun around in her arms and faced her.

"If you promise that you'll bring me back here sometime." Bree smiled and wrapped her arms around Carson's waist.

Carson pulled Bree in tight against her chest. "Anything."

Carson led Bree back to the truck and helped her into the seat. She watched Carson make her way around the vehicle and was overcome with an unfamiliar joy. As Bree's heart soared, her thoughts flashed to Marion, and the joy that had just consumed her vanished. She stared out the window as memories of the past flooded her mind, and Bree felt an all-too-familiar tightening in her chest.

What are you doing? What if Marion came home tomorrow and here you are in the arms of another woman? Bree couldn't imagine what Marion would say if she ever discovered that Bree had been carrying on with another woman behind her back. *It's not behind her back, Bree. She's gone. She's never coming back, and you know it.* But Bree didn't know it, not really. She had hung on to those words of promise when Marion told her she would return. *What about Carson? You're leading her on and getting all this attention, and then what?* The last thing she wanted to do was to hurt

Carson. Bree's chest tightened and her breaths grew quick and shallow.

Marion had left her, without concern or remorse. How could she continue to hold on to someone who could abandon someone they *loved* with such carelessness? Yet, there Carson was, treating her with more thoughtfulness in one single gesture than Bree had ever gotten in years of marriage. Her heart clenched in her chest.

When Carson slid into the truck, Bree pressed her eyes closed. She didn't want Carson to see the conflicting emotions that warred within her. Just as the wave of anxiety threatened to consume her, Carson took her hand. Bree glanced over at the strong hand that held hers. Her eyes followed as Carson brought her hand up and kissed her fingers. The pressure that had threatened to squeeze every last breath from Bree's lungs eased as Carson smiled at her. It was a kind smile full of happiness and serenity.

They drove down the mountain into town. Bree could only stare over at Carson's striking profile. Bree's chest, once filled up with guilt and sorrow, now allowed room for a sliver of hopefulness and excitement. She remembered the comfort she'd felt with Carson's strong, protective arms wrapped around her. There was something so right about how she felt pressed up against Carson, like nothing in the world mattered except the passion and desire that burned between them. It was when they touched that everything else seemed so insignificant. Bree forced herself to hold on to that feeling.

She let her mind drift further with contentment and fell into a fantasy full of flesh and heat. Her pulse quickened as she fell into the desires of her mind. Bree wanted to feel Carson's bare skin on hers. She wanted to run her fingers over the soft swells of her breasts, down her belly, and glide them into the warm wet folds between her legs. Just the thought of being inside Carson made Bree wet. The vehicle came to a stop, and Bree was jolted from her fantasy. She blinked herself back to reality and saw that Carson stared back at her.

"I don't know where you were, but I've never wanted to be there more than I do right now," Carson said as she leaned over toward Bree.

"I was just…I was daydreaming, I guess you could call it." Bree's face flushed.

"I wish I was part of that daydream." Carson cupped Bree's face in her hand and stroked her cheek with her thumb.

"Believe me, you were." Bree touched the hand on her cheek and closed the space between their lips. She kissed Carson gently, but didn't allow the kiss to linger. There was a perfect possibility that she wouldn't have stopped herself from picking up where her fantasy had left off. And it was not the right time, for several reasons. Bree took a deep breath and exhaled. "Are we here? We should go. Yes?" Bree moved Carson's hand down to her lap and tapped it a few times before letting it go.

Carson looked from her hand to Bree. "What? Oh, right. Yes. We should go."

❖

Jim looked at his watch for what might have been the twentieth time in just ten minutes. Bree and Carson were expected to arrive at any moment. He glanced around at the few close friends that were invited to surprise Bree for her birthday. It made him happy that she had such a great group of people who loved her and wanted to spend the evening with her. There wasn't a large number of them, five plus Bree and Carson. He stood in the doorway of the private dining room that Carson had rented and peeked out into the restaurant to look for his little girl and her date.

When he heard a burst of laughter, his attention turned to Barbara, who stood with Suzanne, Gwen, Alan, and his partner. Barbara had her hand to her chest as she and the others laughed at something hilarious that Alan had said. Jim adored when Barbara smiled and even more so when she laughed. He'd known Barbara for many years, yet it seemed as though he'd just begun to see her. He found himself going out of his way to casually check in with her throughout the workday. He'd also begun thinking of random and nonsensical ideas or topics to bring to her attention as if he were unable to proceed without her essential input. He realized what he was doing when he brought her an audio wand and asked her what he should do with it. To his relief she thought he was just being silly, and he was so dumbfounded by his realization that he just played along. Either she had caught on and was saving him from shame or she found it charming. Either way, he cherished her all the more for it.

It was the first time that Jim and Barbara had seen each other outside of work. It wasn't that he hadn't wanted to ask her out, maybe to dinner or coffee, he just didn't know how to do it, or more importantly if he should. Jim had found himself attracted to other women since Juliet died. Yet a part of him never felt that the timing or the woman was right.

The maître d' slipped into the room and signaled that Bree and Carson had arrived. He then slipped away and shut the door behind him. The six of them grouped together and faced the door. In his excitement, Jim wrapped his arm around Barbara's waist and pulled her close to his side. The door opened and the maître d' reappeared followed by Bree and Carson. Jim realized what he had done as he released her to welcome a very surprised Bree.

Everyone clapped and smiled. Bree covered her mouth in amazement while tears filled her eyes. Carson stroked her arms, and Jim couldn't help but notice Carson's loving gesture. He reached out for his girls and hugged them both. "Happy birthday, sweetheart," he said as he squeezed them both in his arms.

"This is wonderful. Whose idea was this?" Bree asked as she looked back and forth between Jim and Carson. They each raised an accusatory finger and pointed to the other. "Well, it's amazing."

Jim watched as Carson stared at Bree in a way he had never seen anyone look at another person. He was overjoyed by the love he saw in her eyes for Bree. "It was all her idea," Jim said as he tweaked Carson's chin. He wanted Carson to take all of the credit for bringing the light back into Bree's life. "Let's get this party started, shall we?" Jim cleared the frog in his throat and rubbed them both on the arm. He looped Bree's arm through his before he led them over to her other waiting guests.

❖

Bree stood on her doorstep and watched as Carson pulled away. Every single part of her body cursed at her mind for not inviting her in. She wanted her; there was no doubt. The night had been perfect—the romantic sunset, the surprise dinner, and the amazing woman who planned it all. But Bree couldn't seem to shake the earlier feeling of gloom when thoughts of Marion rushed to her mind. At one of Bree's happiest moments, the memories of her past had ripped it away from her. Bree was overwhelmed with a variety of emotions that ranged from anxiety and anger to sadness and remorse. More painful than the feelings she had for Marion were the same ones battling in her heart for Carson. Unable to hold it back any longer, she cried. Bree leaned back against the wall of her porch with her face in her hands and sobbed.

She slid down the wall and held her legs against her chest as she cried. She cried for the loss of Marion, for the guilt she had at the idea of moving on without her, and she cried for the uncontrollable feelings that she was developing for Carson. Bree had decided many years earlier that she could never love another person the way she had loved Marion, and she could never allow herself to put all her faith and trust into someone else again. But now she found herself thinking about another woman in order to pull herself out of the sadness of her memories. Carson was so attentive and kind that Bree didn't know how she'd ever existed without knowing such a kind heart. She could no longer remember any of the ways that Marion had made her happy. Bree didn't know if they never existed or if Carson had washed them all away.

Bree hadn't heard anyone approach, so when she felt a hand on her shoulder she gasped and flung her head up. While she was embarrassed to have been caught, she was relieved that it was her uncle and not Carson. When she recognized his face through the fog of her tears, she threw her arms around his neck and cried harder.

"Breezy…kiddo. What's wrong, sweetheart? What happened?" Jim held her close and stroked her hair as she trembled. "Shh. It's okay. Bree, look at me." He cooed at her and tried to calm her enough for her to talk. When she said nothing and continued to weep, he picked her up into his arms and carried her inside.

❖

Jim laid her down on the couch and covered her with a blanket. He sat on the edge and rubbed her back until she spoke. "Marion. She ruined everything."

Jim looked down at Bree confused. "Marion? Don't you mean Carson?"

Bree looked up at Jim with her tear stained face. "No. Marion. Carson is wonderful."

"Baby girl, Marion isn't here. She's gone. She can't ruin anything." Jim had waited for this moment. He was sure she'd had moments like this before she'd gotten home, but this was the first time he had experienced it.

"She ruined my birthday. She did it on purpose. I know it." Bree pushed her face into the pillow. "She doesn't want me, but she doesn't want me to be happy either. Why can't I hate her?"

"Your birthday isn't ruined. It was a beautiful birthday. You were so happy tonight, sweetheart, so much happier than I've ever seen you. Carson adores you. Can you see the way she looks at you? No one and nothing can take that away."

Bree's sobs slowed, and she looked up at him. "It was so beautiful, wasn't it? She gave me the best birthday I've ever had." Bree started to tear up again. "And I sent her away tonight, because of Marion. I gave her my heart, and I never got it back. How can I even think about giving it to someone else? I'm a horrible person."

"Shh. It's okay. You're a beautiful and wonderful person, and you know it. Don't worry about that right now. Let's talk about the good things."

"Good things. Okay. Well, she took me up Town Mountain Road to watch the sunset over downtown. It was so beautiful." Bree sat up and her head swirled. "Oh…maybe not," she said before she lay back down, this time on Jim's lap. "You should've seen it. The sky and clouds were just so gorgeous and the lights of the city sparkled. The way she wrapped her arms around me was like nothing I've ever felt before."

"It sounds beautiful, my love," Jim said as he stroked her hair. It was just as he remembered doing so many times while she was growing up. He would pet her head and encourage her to talk about the positive points of something until she fell asleep on his lap. He looked down and realized that although she was older now, it still worked like a charm. Bree's eyes were closed and her breaths were soft and steady. She was sound asleep. He sat with her a while longer, until he was ready to leave her alone.

CHAPTER SIXTEEN

Bree's eyes flickered open and she glanced around the room. It took her several seconds to figure out where she was. She sat up, rubbed her face, and pulled back hands covered in the streaked remnants of her makeup from the night before. She pushed herself off the couch and into a stiff but standing position and noticed that she still had on her beautiful red gown. "I'm such a mess." Bree stripped her dress off over her head before she headed up the stairs to her room.

When she reached the top step, the doorbell rang. "Seriously?" she said as she looked down at herself in nothing except her panties. "One sec," she yelled as she sprinted into her bedroom and grabbed the robe off the bedpost. She slipped it on and tied the belt around her waist as she hurried back down the steps. When she reached the door, she unlocked it and flung it open. "Good mor—oh my God," she yelped and slammed the door shut. It was not Jim, as she expected. It was Carson.

Bree could hear Carson laugh on the other side of the door as she said, "Good morning to you, too, beautiful."

Bree tried to tame her wild bed head and wipe away some of the mascara that was no doubt smeared over her entire face. She cursed herself for not having a mirror by the front door.

It was hopeless, and she couldn't just let Carson stand on her front porch, so she opened the door again, but only a sliver. "Hi."

"Aww…Hi, babe." Carson leaned in toward the crack that Bree pressed her forehead to. "Expecting someone else?"

"Yes. Well, no. Not exactly. I just assumed you were my uncle."

"Oh. Well, I hope I didn't disappoint you. I could go get him if you like." Carson winked before she turned to leave.

Bree flung open the door. "No. Don't go." Carson had no real intention of leaving, of course, and Bree played right into it.

Carson turned back toward Bree and froze, her eyes wide. "Um, maybe we should go inside?"

Bree followed Carson's wide gaze down to where her robe open and plunged into a deep V to expose the soft curves of her breasts. Bree gasped and clutched the fabric closed over her chest. Her face burned red and she hung her head in embarrassment. "This just keeps getting better."

Carson moved in closer and put her hands on Bree's arms. She rubbed up and down as she bowed her head to look up at Bree. "Hey, you are the most beautiful thing I could ever wish to see in the morning. Come on." Carson guided Bree backward into the house and closed the door behind them. "Look at me." Carson placed her fingers under Bree's chin and lifted her head. "You're beautiful. Now, I'll make some coffee while you go get dressed, okay?"

Bree fell into Carson's sky blue eyes and smiled. "Okay. I'll be right back." Bree turned and headed up the stairs to fix the disaster that she was.

❖

Carson found the coffee easily enough and started to brew an extra-strong pot. Bree was a beautiful woman, but it was clear that her disheveled appearance that morning went beyond a usual tousled morning look. There wasn't any doubt that Bree had cried the night before, and it worried Carson. She was lost in thought as she watched the coffee drip. She hoped that Bree trusted her enough to ask for help if she needed it. When she heard the shower start, she got an idea. Carson was going to cook breakfast. She went to the refrigerator and gathered up everything she would need to make a delicious surprise for Bree.

Carson poured the coffee and set out the plates just as Bree entered the kitchen. "I smell bacon."

Carson looked up and stopped in mid-motion. "Wow," was all she could say when Bree appeared. Her hair was still wet and her face was clear and bright from the shower.

Bree stopped in front of a paralyzed Carson and snatched a small piece of bacon from one of the plates. "Much better," she said before she popped the crispy bit into her mouth. "Look at you, making breakfast. Too bad it's not in bed." Bree winked as she took the plates from Carson and set them on the table.

Before she turned back around, Carson was pressed up against her back. She wrapped her arms around Bree's waist, and Bree rested her head on Carson's shoulder. Carson kissed her exposed neck and tasted her fresh, sweet skin. It didn't take long before Carson's appetite grew for something much more satisfying than bacon and hash browns.

"Mmm." Bree moaned as Carson nibbled from her ear to her shoulder. Spurred on by the sound, Carson slid her hand down Bree's belly, but she was stopped short when her hand was pulled back up to Bree's waist and held there. "The bacon is going to get cold," Bree said without moving from the embrace.

Carson felt that whatever had bothered Bree through the night was still there. She squeezed her and without words tried to let her know that she was with her. Carson rested her chin on Bree's shoulder and kissed her neck. "Let's eat."

As they sat to eat, Carson brought up the real reason she'd come over, and it wasn't just for the opportunity to catch Bree in all of her morning glory. "So, I was thinking. I remember hearing about how much you enjoyed horseback riding." Carson couldn't help but laugh when Bree looked up wide-eyed with a piece of bacon sticking out of her mouth. "Right. So, I went and made reservations at the stables for eleven o'clock today. If you're interested, of course."

Bree stuffed the rogue meat into her mouth and jumped up from her seat. "Really? That would be wonderful." She threw herself across Carson's lap and draped her arms around her neck. "I'd love to go riding with you today," Bree said before she pressed her salty lips against Carson's.

They finished breakfast and then Carson made Bree go get dressed while she cleaned up the kitchen. She was glad that Bree accepted her proposal for a day at the stables and even more so that she had helped put the smile back on Bree's beautiful face. Carson licked her lips, which still tasted like Bree's salty sweetness, and she smiled.

❖

Bree loved the Pine Creek Stables. It was a gorgeous drive over the mountains and around Lake Lure to get there. It was the type of place that Bree imagined owning one day. It had beautiful fishing lakes, hundreds of acres of riding trails and pastureland, gorgeous barns, and a small working farm with a bed-and-breakfast. It was a fantasy she'd almost forgotten about until they pulled onto the long gravel road that weaved through the property. Carson pulled into a spot alongside a barn with a large "Welcome Y'all!" sign.

Bree looked over at Carson with an enormous smile that she made no attempt to hide. "Are you ready?" Carson flashed an anxious smile and nodded before Bree jumped out of the truck.

As rustic and natural as it was, Bree loved the smell of being on a farm. She linked her arm with Carson and dragged her along as she skipped into the barn. They were greeted by two trail guides who handed them identical clipboards with the obligatory "you can't sue us if you die" forms. They sat on a long wooden bench where another couple already sat. Bree zipped through her list of checkboxes and signed her name on the bottom line. She looked over at Carson, who hunched over her clipboard and studied each statement before she checked the corresponding box. Bree was about to make a goofy comment about t's and i's until it hit her. She leaned over Carson's clipboard and looked up at her. "Have you ever done this before?"

Carson shrugged her shoulders up to her ears, and her cheeks turned pink. "Um, not exactly."

"Aww. You've never been on a horse before?" Bree asked as Carson turned to face her.

"Well, honestly, no."

Bree found her innocence the most adorable and heartwarming thing she'd ever seen. Carson was willing to do something she had never done just because Bree liked to do it. *Marion would have nev—No.* Bree refused to let her steal another moment from her and Carson. "We don't have—"

"Absolutely not. We are going. I want to go," Carson cut Bree off in mid-sentence.

It was not a negotiation, and that was more than fine with Bree. She was now even more elated about being there with Carson to share a new experience with her. "Yes, ma'am. Then finish that form, and let's go."

They finished their forms and listened as the guides led them through the very basics of horsemanship and trail riding. Carson seemed a bit more at ease with the experience once she realized they weren't going to strap her onto a wild mustang, slap its ass, and send her racing over the mountains. That was until they were led out to the stalls and presented with their equine partners. Bree watched Carson while she stared in bewilderment as the guides picked through the group and assigned them each to a horse. They called Bree forward and paired her with a large white mare named Momma, and she smiled back at Carson, who still waited patiently to be chosen. Bree stood next to her mare as the guides double-checked the buckles and straps. Once she got the all clear, she slipped her foot into the stirrup and heaved herself onto Momma's back. She looked back just as a cowboy called Carson forward. "We're gonna put you on big Jack. He's o'er there," he drawled as he pointed at the end of the row toward a large black stallion that towered over the rest of the team.

Carson flashed a look of shock as she walked past Bree whose own mouth was gaped open in surprise. Bree covered her mouth with her hand as she watched Carson being led over to the enormous black stallion. By the look on Carson's face, the horse may as well have been a guillotine. Bree couldn't see what was happening at the far end where Carson prepared to mount her horse, so she couldn't help but feel a little nervous for her. When Carson popped up at the end of the row and onto her horse, Bree giggled at the look of pure excitement and pride on Carson's face. She beamed from ear to ear, and Bree couldn't see any of the anxiety that she'd had when they first arrived.

The trail guides led each horse out one by one. They kept the couples together and arranged their horses in the line accordingly. Bree and Carson were the last two to join the line, and Jack took his place at the rear.

They rode through the creeks and trails and stopped from time to time when one of the horses ahead decided it would stop for a trailside snack or a sip from the creek. Jack took every opportunity available to put on the brakes in the middle of every stream they crossed. As instructed, Carson attempted to prevent his water breaks, but she proved no match for Jack's robust and determined wants. Bree's mare, on the other hand, was far less motivated. Oftentimes she slowed to a near stop, content to nap and wait for someone to come and pick her up on the way back. Bree gave up trying to motivate Momma with kicks and thrusts early on. At every opportunity she had, Bree glanced back to see the amusement that was still affixed to Carson's face. The ride itself was a wonderful surprise, but the real gift Carson had given her was the hope Bree felt every time she looked at her.

❖

Carson pulled up and stopped at Jim's house as Bree had requested. As Carson hopped out of the vehicle, her knees buckled and she almost dissolved into a gelatinous heap on the ground. There was no way she could have played it off. As soon as she heard Bree roar with laughter she knew there wasn't even a point. Carson leaned on the truck seat until she felt she had enough control over her legs to walk. She watched as Bree jumped out of the truck without even a flinch. Carson was a little jealous until she saw Bree round the front of the truck walking like she still had a horse between her legs. They each burst into hysterical laughter at the sad sight of the other. Carson closed the door of her truck and limped behind Bree to the kitchen door. Each of them cried a painful "ooh" or "ow" or "shit" with each step they took. Bree knocked on the door and waited for her uncle to answer.

"What the hell happened to you girls?" he asked as he opened the door and let them in. His nose scrunched up as they walked past him into the house.

"Carson took me horseback riding at Pine Creek. It was wonderful," Bree said as she wobbled to the kitchen table and plopped down on the seat. "Ow!"

Carson cringed because she knew Bree would regret sitting on the hard chair before she'd even done it.

"Okay. Well, I guess I should head out," Carson said as she motioned to the door behind her.

"No, don't go. I mean, why don't you stay for dinner?"

"Well, I need to shower off some of this barn smell." Carson noticed the look of disappointment on Bree's face and added, "But I can pick something up on the way back?"

"Yes. I mean, if that's okay with you, Uncle Jim?"

Jim looked at them. "Ha! Like my answer would even matter? Of course it's okay."

Carson leaned down and kissed Bree on the lips. "I'll see you soon, sweetheart."

CHAPTER SEVENTEEN

While Carson and Jim sat hypnotized by the television, Bree got up from the couch. She gathered the wrappers and remnants of the Chinese takeout dinner they'd devoured. Carson offered to help, but Bree refused. "No. I've got it. You sit and watch the show. I have to get off my broken ass anyway." Bree gave Carson a quick peck on the lips and then took the trash to the kitchen.

She wasn't surprised that there weren't any leftovers. Carson and Jim could eat enough for a family of four when they got together. She guessed they would've eaten the packaging had they been able to digest Styrofoam. *Edible takeout packaging, now there's an idea*, she thought before she tossed the trash in the can and put the dirty utensils in the dishwasher. When she returned from the kitchen, Carson stared at the TV, but Jim fidgeted with his cell phone and stared off into space.

Bree sat next to Carson and tapped her on the leg. "Hey. What's wrong with him?" She motioned in her uncle's direction.

Carson looked over. "Oh, I have no idea." She reached for the remote and turned off the television. "Hey, Jimbo. What's going on, man? Why the newspaper face?"

Bree looked at Carson and asked, "Newspaper face?"

Carson laughed. "Yeah, it's better than calling it poop face."

"Ewww. What the…?"

Now Jim laughed. "That's a good one, too."

Bree shook her head and waved her hand. "Don't tell me. I don't want to know." She blinked several times. She hoped to erase the imagery associated with her uncle and his private bathroom moments.

Carson rubbed Bree's shoulders and laughed. "So, Jimbo, what's up? Waiting for a call?" She motioned to the phone he flipped over and over in his hands.

"Yeah, well, no. Okay, listen, I need to run something by you and I want to know what you think. Okay?" He looked at Bree, and her heart started to race.

"Oh my God. What's wrong? Are you sick? What happened?" Bree scooted to the edge of the couch.

Carson stood up. "Hey, um, I'm gonna go so you guys can—" She began to excuse herself, but Jim interrupted.

"No, sit. I want your opinion, too, Car."

Carson dropped back down and put her hand on Bree's thigh. "Okay, I'm here."

Jim looked down at his phone and back up to Bree and Carson. "I don't know where to start, so here goes. When your aunt Juliet died, it was pretty rough. I wasn't sure from day to day whether I could or wanted to keep going."

Bree remembered all the nights she had heard him crying in his bedroom. "But you did, and I'm so grateful for that." Bree touched his knee as she strained to hold back her tears.

"So am I, sweetheart." Jim smiled at her. "You were all that I had left, and I swore I would love you and only you for the rest of my life."

"And I love you," Bree said. No longer able to restrain her emotion, she let the tears fall.

"Oh, don't cry, my love. It's okay." Jim patted her hand and reassured her. "Dammit, this ain't going the way I thought…I guess what I'm trying to say is…I've met someone. And I want your—"

"What?" Bree and Carson both blurted out in surprise. They all sat in silence for what seemed like an eternity.

"I've met someone," Jim repeated. "And I wanted to make sure you were okay with it first. Before I ask her out."

Bree squeezed Carson's leg and stood up. She paced in front of the coffee table while Carson sat back in silence. "So let me get this right. You've met someone. A woman. And you want my permission to date her."

"Yes," Jim said as he shifted to the edge of his chair and put his phone down on the table. "Bree, I—"

"Who is she? Where did you meet her? How long has this been going on?" Bree stopped pacing and put her hands on her hips.

Jim stood. "We met at work. It's—"

Carson let out the chuckle that she'd been trying to conceal. Jim raised his eyebrow at her and then glanced back when he heard Bree giggle. Her stern expression cracked with an uncontrollable grin.

Jim stood in confusion and glanced back and forth between them until Bree came over and hugged him.

"Don't you ever scare me like that again." Bree pulled away and held his hands in hers. "And if you dare tell us that this someone isn't Barbara, then I'm afraid I will not give my blessing." Bree and Carson both burst into laughter when Jim's mouth dropped open in shock.

"But…how?" He stuttered.

"Seriously, Jimbo? A person would have to be blind not to see the way the two of you look at each other." Carson said it before Bree could.

Bree agreed. "Yeah, it's disgusting."

"Dammit. I love you kids." Jim pulled Carson up by her arm and wrapped both of them into a bear hug.

Bree pretended to gasp for air. "Okay. Okay. Now I think someone has a phone call to make. Don't you?" Bree looked at Carson and nodded.

"Yes. We should go." Carson pointed to the back door.

Bree laughed. "We should." Bree kissed her uncle on the cheek and grabbed Carson by the arm. She dragged her through the house as they shouted their good-byes to Jim.

Once they'd made it out the back door and onto the driveway, they continued laughing. Carson grabbed Bree into her arms and lifted her off the ground. "That was great."

"That'll teach him to make me cry like that."

Carson set Bree back down. "Yeah. I almost had to kick his ass for that one."

"Aww, you'd do that for me?" Bree blinked with exaggerated sweetness.

"I'd do anything for you, Bree Whitley." Carson kissed her softly.

The words lit a fire inside Bree, and she kissed Carson back with a fierce desire unlike any she'd felt before. Bree sucked on Carson's lip, which elicited a deep moan of desire. The sound fueled the heat that burned low in her belly. When Carson's tongue touched hers, she felt an instant rush between her legs. "Come home with me?"

Carson didn't answer, but she didn't pull away when Bree grabbed her hand and led her up the hill to the house.

❖

Carson followed Bree into the dark house as her heart pounded in her chest. Carson kicked the door closed behind her before she wrapped her arms around Bree and claimed her mouth for her own. Carson needed to feel Bree's skin on hers. She wanted to lick every inch of Bree's body. She'd imagined so many times how she would work her way down from her neck to settle in the warmth between her thighs. Carson kissed Bree's neck and Bree moaned with pleasure. Carson was wet. She knew Bree was, too, and she needed to feel it. Carson slid her hands down Bree's back and pulled their bodies together as she pressed her thigh between Bree's legs. Bree gasped.

Wrapped together, Bree guided Carson backward until they reached the couch. Carson lowered Bree down and hovered over her as her eyes plotted out the path that her tongue would take. She straddled Bree's hips and sat back on her own legs as she memorized the body under her. Bree ran her hands over Carson's chest. She teased her nipples to tight peaks through the thin material. Carson was thankful she rarely ever wore a bra. As Bree unbuttoned Carson's shirt, her pulse and breath quickened. She tried to refrain from pressing herself down onto Bree but failed when Bree raised her hips to make first contact. Carson shuddered as the stiff seam of her jeans pressed into her clit. Bree released the last button and opened her shirt to expose her breasts. Before Carson could wish for Bree's warm mouth to be on her, Bree sat up and took one of Carson's nipples into her mouth. Carson's head fell back as she offered herself up for Bree to devour.

She needed to touch Bree and feel her smooth heat. Carson slipped her hand between them to the button on Bree's jeans. In one swift motion, she had the button and zipper open to allow room for her hand to slide into Bree's panties. "You are so wet."

Bree's head fell back as Carson eased her fingers into the smooth folds. "Oh, God."

Carson positioned herself between Bree's legs. She leaned

down over Bree. "You feel so good." Carson cupped Bree in her hand and slid a finger inside her as she licked the side of Bree's neck.

Carson slid another finger into Bree and pulsed them in and out. Bree's hips bucked and Carson matched the rhythm that Bree set. She was close. Carson could feel it.

"Carson, stop."

"What?" Carson asked, thinking she'd heard wrong.

"Please. Stop," Bree said.

Carson pulled her hand back as Bree attempted to sit. Carson sat up to allow Bree room to move. "What's wrong? Did I hurt you?" Carson reached out for Bree's face and felt the tears on her cheek.

"You're crying." Carson pulled Bree into her arms.

"I'm okay," Bree said as she pressed her head against Carson's chest.

"Baby, look at me." Carson lifted Bree's chin with two fingers and looked into her eyes. "What's going on?"

Bree closed her eyes as the tears streamed down her face.

"Shh, it's okay," Carson cooed as she rocked a weeping Bree in her arms. She had no idea why Bree was upset, and she didn't know what else to do but hold her. They sat in the silent darkness for a while until Carson suggested that she leave so Bree could get into bed.

"Don't leave. Will you stay with me? Hold me for a while?" Bree asked.

"Anything, remember?"

❖

Bree stood at the edge of her bed and brushed her wet hair when Carson came up behind her. "Hey." Bree turned around to see Carson there with a steaming mug.

"I made you some tea," she said before she set it on the nightstand.

Bree smiled. "Thank you. Oh, I got you something to wear. It's in the bathroom. There are towels, too, if you want to shower. You don't have to. I was just…"

Carson touched Bree's face. "Thank you."

Carson went to the bathroom to shower and change while Bree slipped into bed. She was embarrassed about what had happened and more than a little frightened that Carson thought she was a nutcase or worse, a tease. She sipped her tea while she waited for Carson to return.

When the bathroom door opened, Bree set her cup down and shifted to make room for Carson. "It's not my style," Carson said as she stood in the doorway and pulled the pink duck print pajama pants out to the sides. "I've always considered myself more of a little piggies kinda girl."

Bree couldn't help but giggle. She'd already laughed when she picked them out of the drawer for Carson, but seeing her in them was even better. "Pink is totally your color."

Carson skipped over to the bed and scooted in. Bree barely waited for Carson to get settled before she pulled Carson's arm around her neck and rested her head on her chest. "This is nice."

"Yes, it is."

"I'm sorry about earlier."

Carson stroked Bree's hair. "Don't be sorry. It's okay."

"No. It's not. I don't want you to think I'm a tease or a prude or whatever."

"Hey." Carson kissed Bree on the top of the head. "I don't think any of those things. I—"

"Wait, let me finish." Bree had to get it off her chest. She wanted to be open and honest with Carson, and this was her chance to put it all on the table. "I came home because I couldn't stay in Boston any longer. It was too hard to live the life I'd planned for two without the other person. I kept living in our house, driving our car, shopping at our stores. She was gone, and I was living like a ghost in a life that didn't exist anymore. I kept waiting for her to come home, and I know that I'd still be waiting if I hadn't come back here."

"I understand." Carson wrapped both arms around Bree.

"I was still waiting for her even after I got here. But then… then I met you and I started to forget what I was waiting for. In the beginning, I felt guilty, like I was betraying her. But now I feel angry. I'm angry that I still allow her to affect my life even though she's no longer in it, and I'm angry that even in my happiest moments she appears in my mind." Bree felt Carson loosen her hold.

"So…tonight. You…you were thinking about her?"

"No. Well, yes. But not like that." Carson sat up. "Wait. I was thinking about how amazing it felt to be with you and how happy I was when I got scared. I can't go through that again, Carson. I barely made it to the other side. It almost killed me." Bree had begun to cry.

Carson pulled Bree into her chest. "Shh, I'm so sorry. It's okay." She held Bree until she fell asleep.

CHAPTER EIGHTEEN

When Bree woke the next morning, Carson was gone. She sat up and felt a quick surge of sadness followed by the fear that she had scared Carson off with her antics the night before. She threw herself back down, buried her face in the pillow, and groaned. She opened her eyes without lifting her head up. Bree spotted a small yellow flower taped to a note that rested on top of a pair of crisp, folded duck print pajamas. She smiled and reached for the flower.

> *My dearest Bree,*
> *You are so beautiful when you sleep it pains me to wake you. I ran home to get ready for work, but I'll see you soon, sweetheart. I miss you already and can't wait to see your face again.*
> *Love,*
> *C*

Bree smiled. She had never been more anxious to get up and get to work than she was at that moment. She hopped up and sped across the room to the bathroom. When the doorbell rang, Bree's heart leapt in her chest. She rinsed the toothpaste from her mouth and grabbed her hairbrush as she slipped into her robe. "She came back." Bree was so glad that Carson decided to come back without her even asking. She trotted out of her closet and the bell chimed again. "I'm coming," she hollered down the stairs. Before she opened the door, Bree checked her face and ran the brush through her hair on her way to the door. Just as she reached it, the bell rang again. "Hold on, babe. I'm right—" Bree froze as she flung open the front door.

Bree's mouth dropped open and the brush she held fell to the floor. Her ears rang and her head swam. She put a death grip on the doorknob, but she wasn't even certain she was still standing. Her entire body was numb. "Marion."

Marion smiled. "Hey, baby."

Bree's heart pounded in her chest and her stomach somersaulted. "What…why…what are you doing…here?" Bree stammered as she forced herself to speak as tears began to fill her eyes.

"I wanted, no, I needed to see you. I've missed you, Breezy." Marion stepped forward and Bree stumbled back. "Are you not happy to see me?"

"No. I mean yes." Bree struggled to keep breathing as her vision blurred. This couldn't be happening. It was a dream. Marion was standing on her front step. She came home. Bree's head was spinning. "Yes." Bree flung her arms open and wrapped them around Marion.

"I've missed you."

Bree buried her face in Marion's neck, "I never thought I'd see you again." Her legs were weak and she felt light-headed. If Marion's arm hadn't gripped at her waist she might have slumped to the ground. "I've missed you so much, Carson."

Marion pulled back and looked down at Bree. "Who?"

Bree looked up at Marion with confusion. "What?"

"You called me Carson. Who is that?"

Her stomach knotted at the realization. *Carson.* Bree stepped back from Marion and clutched her robe. "She... she's my...a friend. Sorry, I don't know why I called you that. Weird." Bree chuckled, hoping to laugh off the slip.

"Oh. Okay. So, can I come in? I'm sure you're cool in that robe. We can talk." Marion reached out and touched Bree's arm.

Bree's skin tingled under Marion's long-forgotten touch. The familiar hand felt foreign after so many years. Marion stepped forward, but Bree backed away. "Wait."

"Bree, baby. It's me."

Bree had waited for this every moment since the day Marion left. Her body began to shake and anxiety boiled within her. She held up her finger to Marion. "I can't. I need...I need to think. I can't think." Bree had wished and prayed every night for two years that this day would come, but now she found herself overwhelmed by it.

"Don't think, my love." Marion reached for Bree's face.

Bree closed her eyes as Marion cupped her face and pressed her soft, warm lips to Bree's. She never thought she'd feel those strong, familiar lips on hers again. Her heart raced as Marion drew her into a longing embrace. "Oh, Marion. You're here."

"I am, sweetheart. I promised."

I promise. A wave of nausea washed over Bree, and she stepped away again. Bree reached for the door behind her and grabbed the knob. "I...I have to go. You should go."

"What?"

"I need some time right now. To think. Jim is going to be up any minute, and I don't want him to find you here. Like this." The last thing she needed was for Jim to see Marion on her front stoop, period, let alone kissing her. Bree stepped backward into the house. And what if Carson came back? "You have to go, now. Please."

"Will you meet me later? I want to talk to you about some things. About us." Marion leaned down and gave Bree a sweet kiss. "I've missed you so much, beautiful."

Bree's stomach twisted. *Us.* Bree was reluctant, but agreed to meet Marion at a local café later that evening. Bree closed the door and rested her head against it as she listened to Marion's car drive away. When she pushed away from the door and turned around, the room whirled around her. Bree grabbed the wall for support and let the tears fall. Bree's mind was in overdrive and she couldn't string any sensible thoughts together. Her wish had come true. Marion had come home.

❖

After Marion left, Bree stumbled her way to her bedroom and sat in the dark on the edge of her bed. Bree was overwhelmed with a variety of emotions that ranged from anxiety and anger to sadness and remorse. She pulled the blanket around her shoulders and curled onto her side and slept.

Bree sat in the middle of the floor in the living room as she watched Marion leave. "I'll be back, I promise." The door closed with a thud, and she was gone. Bree heard a loud rumble, and the walls began to shake. The frames and shelves vibrated as the walls began to move. Bree looked around her as the four walls started to slide in toward her. The walls shook violently. She watched as frames and shelves came loose and fell to the floor. She watched as pictures and memories from her life crashed and shattered around her. She refused to move, even if she could have. Bree would wait. Marion would come home.

As the walls grew closer to Bree, panic and claustrophobia set in. "Hurry. Marion, please save me," she begged as she held her arms out toward the approaching walls. She extended her legs out straight. She might not stop them, but she would slow them down. She had to give Marion more time. The windows shattered and sent shards of glass raining down over her. The room shrank more and the light from the outside began to dim. Bree held her arms out and pushed her palms to the walls with all her strength. She screamed for Marion, but she did not come.

Bree struggled to stop the walls from crushing her. She knew that no matter how hard she tried, her strength alone was not enough to stop them. "Marion, I tried." She dropped her arms as the light that remained pinched into a slender beam. She closed her eyes and resigned herself to fate as the air in the room grew hot and thick. Bree closed her eyes and waited for her inevitable end from the crushing weight around her. If she couldn't escape, she hoped that it would end quickly. She held her breath as she prepared herself.

Suddenly, the tiny space was silent. The rumble of the moving walls had ceased. She opened her eyes but saw the faint illuminated presence of legs braced against the walls. "Marion." Bree knew she would come. She exhaled a sigh of relief as two strong arms reached down and drew her up from the small dark space. They cradled her against them before they jerked her free from the room. Bree watched as the walls lurched forward and slammed closed around what would have been her body. Bree felt a soft kiss on her forehead before she looked up at her hero.

Carson.

❖

Two loud knocks startled Bree awake. She had not expected Jim to be standing a few feet away at her bedroom door holding two cups of coffee. She jolted upright and threw off the covers. "Holy shit! You scared the crap out of me."

Jim's expression was one of concern as he came forward and extended the cup out to her. He twisted his wrist and looked at the watch on his other hand. "Running a little late today?"

Bree took the cup and brought it up to her mouth. "I'm not late, and it's only—" Bree stopped mid-sip when she noticed the time on the stove: 8:07 a.m. "Ooh, well, yeah. I guess so."

"Is everything all right? I called Carson this morning when you two didn't come to the house, and she said that you weren't with her. I got worried and let myself in."

"Okay." Bree felt drained of energy and hadn't really understood anything he'd just said.

"Bree." He held out his hand and touched her forehead.

"I'm fine. Tired, I think." Bree's head was abuzz with a thousand thoughts and none of them made any sense. She set the coffee cup onto her nightstand and curled back up onto her side. "I'm just going to lie here for a while."

Jim sat on the edge of the bed. "Did something…happen with you and Carson?"

"What? No. Nothing happened. We just talked." Bree had never talked to Jim about her sex life before, and she didn't intend to start then. "And this morning, she left. A note. What a wonderful note. She's beautiful, and her handwriting is beautiful, and her words are beautiful." Bree rambled and mumbled nonsensical sentences. "She likes me, I think. Likes, likes me. But she left me. Just like that. And now she's back."

"Bree, I think you're still half asleep and have no idea what you're saying. I know I don't. You go back to sleep, and I'll call Barbara and let her know you won't be in today. Okay?"

"Okay." Bree closed her eyes as Jim kissed her cheek. Her eyes flashed back open as he stood up. "Hey. Did you ask Barbara out on a date?"

Jim laughed. "Yes, sweetheart. We're going to have dinner tonight. Now go back to sleep, and I'll come by and check on you later." He brushed a few stray strands of hair from her forehead.

"Good night," she whispered as she dozed off to sleep.

❖

Carson unlocked the door and headed upstairs to her apartment. Just as she made it up the steel staircase to the loft balcony above, she heard a whistle.

"Ooh, I can't even remember the last time I saw your walk of shame. Looks good, baby."

Carson looked down and saw Kelli. She stood in the middle of the warehouse and whipped a towel around in the air. "Seriously? I can't even remember the last time I saw you awake before noon."

"Ouch. The floozy has jokes," Kelli shot back.

"Back at you. Now leave me alone. I have to go shower and get ready for work." Kelli's laughter continued even as Carson disappeared into her apartment.

❖

Carson showered, dressed, and headed back downstairs. She hoped that Kelli was still around. "Yo. Where you at?" Carson hollered through the expansive room, which was, as always, landscaped with large sculptures in various phases of completion. "Helloooo? Anyone home?"

Kelli peeked out from behind an enormous obelisk. "Are you trying to wake the dead? I'm right here." Kelli snickered and pointed to the stone. "It's a grave marker. See what I did there? Grave, dead…Ugh."

It was funny, but Carson refused to laugh at the joke. She enjoyed it more when Kelli struggled to explain how funny the joke was. "Right. I see. Good one," Carson deadpanned.

"You're such a dick. What do you want?" Kelli grunted and disappeared back behind the monument, peeking back long enough to say, "Can't you see I'm busy?"

"Busting my balls does not count as busy."

"As your best friend, that's my full-time job." Kelli stepped out from behind the block and spread her arms to motion around the room. "All this is what I do to occupy my time before I catch you sneaking back in from wherever you've been all night."

"Oh. Now it makes sense."

"So?" Kelli put her hands on her hips.

"So…what?" Carson stalled her response in order to drive Kelli to the edge.

"Don't give me that shit, you harlot. Where were you last night?" Kelli tapped her foot.

Carson laughed. "You're so easy. You know that?"

"Really? You are going to hand me the ammo now?"

Carson stepped back and hoisted herself up onto a drafting table. "I was with Bree. I stayed at her place last night." Carson reminisced about how perfect it felt to wake up with Bree snuggled against her side as she slept peacefully on her chest.

"Aw, man. I was going to give you crap about that, until you went and made that face." Kelli pointed her finger at Carson and swirled it around.

"What face? I didn't make a face." Carson scoffed.

"That schmoopy, puppy dog, 'I had the most amazing night of my life' face."

"Shut up."

Kelli laughed, and Carson felt her face turn red. She had made the face, but she refused to give Kelli the win. "Whatever. Hey, can I ask you something?"

Kelli's face lost all hints of humor. "Of course." She leaned against the table that Carson sat on.

"Am I doing this right?"

"What do you mean?"

"I don't know. I don't really know what I'm doing. I wake up in the morning, and I can't wait to see her. I go to sleep at night, and I wish that I was with her. I'm not sure whether I'm coming or going, and I can't decide if it's a feeling I love or hate."

"I think for the first time, you are doing it perfectly right. Because you aren't using this"—Kelli tapped her finger to Carson's temple and then to her chest—"you're using this."

Carson contemplated Kelli's words about the use of her heart when her phone vibrated in her pocket. She hopped off the table and dug it out of her jeans hoping it was Bree. When she read the message her stomach filled with butterflies. "Huh. That's weird."

"What is?"

"It's Jim. He asked if Bree was with me because she didn't come up to the house this morning for coffee."

"Maybe you wore her out, and she overslept." Kelli winked and poked an elbow in her direction.

"Kelli. We didn't even do anything. But maybe she did oversleep. I'll just send her a quick text." Carson typed Bree a quick and sweet *Good Morning, beautiful. xoxo.* "Hey, I'm gonna head out and see if I can catch her before she starts her first tour."

"You really like her, don't you?" Kelli flashed Carson a sweet smile.

"I think I do. And now I have to go to work because I need to kiss her right now, and I can't do that if I'm sitting around here with you." Carson hugged Kelli and sprinted out the door as Kelli called after her.

"Kiss her for me, too."

❖

Bree had avoided texts and calls all day from everyone except Jim. She gave him the excuse that she was battling a stomach bug in order to keep him and Carson at bay. Bree sat by the front window and watched as her uncle pulled out of the driveway. Once he disappeared down the road, she waited a few more minutes to make sure he didn't come back. When she felt the all clear, Bree grabbed her keys from the hook and got into her car. She was running late, as she had no choice but to wait for Jim to leave for his date before she could. She felt like a sneaky teenager creeping out of the house after her parents had fallen asleep. It might have been unnecessary, but she didn't want to have to explain herself.

Bree arrived at the restaurant and found Marion seated alone in a secluded corner. Marion smiled at Bree as she approached, and Bree smiled back. It had been so long, and yet she was still the same as Bree remembered. Marion was tall and slender. She was dressed in a fitted black polo and a pair of loose jeans that hung perfectly from her hips. Bree admired her confident physique as she stood and pulled out the chair for her.

Marion sat across from her and smiled again. "You look so great. How have you been?"

Bree blushed. It always made her feel so good when Marion complimented her. "You do, too. I've been good. I'm working at the Biltmore and—"

The waiter arrived with two glasses of wine and set them on the table. "I went ahead and ordered you a glass after you messaged and said you were running late. I hope you don't mind."

Bree didn't mind. As a matter of fact, she was surprised that Marion even remembered what type of wine she liked. "You remembered."

Marion's eyes sparkled, and she flashed a suave smile, "How could I ever forget anything about you? You know, I've thought about you every day, Bree."

The words made Bree's stomach turn over. *She thought about me every day but never once in over two years reached out?* "Oh."

"Have you thought about me?"

Bree couldn't believe she had asked such a ridiculous question. Marion knew Bree well enough to know that she had thought about her every day since she left. Why did she need to hear her say it? She wouldn't tell Marion that it was no less than every hour of every day that she was on her mind. That was until Carson came into her life. Bree answered honestly. "I used to."

"Ouch. Used to?"

Bree took a long sip of her wine. "Yes. It was too hard to keep living that way. I had to start thinking about myself and moving on with my life. I had to learn who I was on my own."

"So you moved here and forgot about me, then."

Bree felt the storm as it built inside her. "I moved here

because you left me. I waited for you, Marion. But then I couldn't do it anymore."

"I know. And I don't know why it's taken me until now to realize what I wanted. I guess I was lost."

"And what do you want?"

"I would think it was obvious."

Bree wanted her to say it. She wanted Marion to say that she wanted her, that she needed her. "It's not."

"I'm here because I want you to come home."

Bree's heart raced. "Come home?"

"Yes. I miss you, and I want us to be together again. We can work together just like we used to. Remember how great that was? We can buy a house outside the city. I don't want to be alone anymore. It can be the two of us, just like it used to be."

Bree grabbed her glass of wine and gulped it down. She could not believe what she heard. It was the very thing that she'd wanted to hear for two long years, but something was wrong. *I'm losing my damn mind. What's wrong with me?* Bree stared into her empty glass.

Marion waved her hand in front of Bree's face. "Bree, sweetheart. Did you hear me?"

Bree blinked and looked up. "Will you excuse me? I need to use the restroom." Bree got up from the table and headed straight for the bathroom. She hoped there would be someone in there willing to slap her awake or check her for stroke symptoms.

She paced in the bathroom. "What the hell is happening? This is everything I've ever hoped for. Why am I not throwing myself at her crying with overwhelming happiness?"

Bree sat on the edge of the small bench near the door. She closed her eyes and put her face into her hands. Why wasn't she saying yes? Bree's phone chimed, and she dug it from her purse.

Hi, babe. Just checking on you. I hope you're feeling better. xoxo -C.

That was why. Bree didn't want to lie to Carson, but she had to respond. *Much better now. Talk to you soon. xoxo -B* Bree slipped her phone back into her purse and headed back to the table.

"I wasn't sure if you were coming back. I take it as a very good sign that you did, though." Marion reached for Bree's hand, but Bree pulled back.

"I wish I could say the same."

❖

Jim and Barbara laughed and flirted over their dinner until she squinted at a familiar figure across the room. Jim followed Barbara's gaze. His eyes widened with surprise when he saw Bree, but his heart seized in his chest when he saw who she sat down with. "Son of a bitch."

"What? Who is that?"

"That…that is the woman who destroyed the only family I have left in the world. Bree's ex, Marion." Jim's ears burned, and he clenched his teeth in seething anger.

"Um. Does Carson know she's here?"

"I doubt it. I didn't even know it." Jim's heart twisted at the thought that Bree had kept this from him and lied to Carson.

"Okay. Well, what do you think she's doing here?" Barbara reached across the table and stroked Jim's arm.

"Nothing good. Of that I'm certain." Jim didn't know why Marion was there. He had no doubt that whatever her reason was, it was based in selfishness and nothing good would come from it.

"Was it that bad? How it ended?"

Jim remembered every last detail of the day Bree called to tell him Marion had left her. He recalled how difficult it was to understand a single word Bree had said through all of the hysterical sobs. His heart ached at the pain in her voice. "Bree wanted a family and Marion wanted success. Even after five years, Marion wasn't ready to settle down. Marion had started to act distant and secretive, so Bree began to suspect she was having an affair. So one day, shortly after their fifth anniversary, Marion came home late and Bree asked if she was seeing someone else. Instead of answering the question, Marion told Bree that she'd taken a position at a museum out in California. Within two weeks, she'd packed her things and was gone. She never once asked Bree to go."

Barbara's eyes filled with tears, and she held her hand over her mouth.

"Bree promised she'd wait as long as she had to. She came into her own during that time and became very self-sufficient. Yet, even with all the learning and distractions, it was all just too much for her. She couldn't shake all the memories and the constant waiting. So after two years of me asking her to come home and start fresh, she finally did. And now…she's here to fuck it all up."

"Aw, sweetheart. You don't know that. Bree is so strong now. Plus, she's in love with Carson."

"Oh, Carson. This will break her heart." Jim's temper flared. Marion had devastated Bree, and now she was going to do it to Carson. He couldn't sit back any longer. He pushed away from the table, and before Barbara could stop him, he stormed over to the table where Bree and Marion sat.

Jim stopped next to the table, and Bree looked up at him in horror. "Uncle Jim! I can explain."

❖

"Hey there, Jim. How's it going?" Marion lifted her glass of wine in greeting.

Jim turned his back on her and directed his attention on Bree.

"We need to talk. Now."

Bree couldn't believe that out of every single restaurant in the entire city, she'd chosen the same one he had. It couldn't have been worse unless Carson had been with him. Her stomach knotted at the possibility and she stood. Bree looked around behind him as she prayed not to see Carson standing there. She sighed with the slightest bit of relief.

"No. She's not with me, if that was who you were looking for."

"She?" Marion peeked around from behind Bree. "She who?"

Jim glowered at Marion. "That is none of your business."

"Oh, I think it is my bu—"

"Enough, both of you." Bree held her hands up between them. "It isn't any of your business," she said to Marion. "We can go outside and discuss this." Bree grabbed Jim by the arm and walked him out to the terrace.

Once they were outside, Jim didn't waste any time before he fired his questions. "Bree, what the hell are you doing? What is Marion doing here?"

"Uncle Jim. Wait. Before you start slamming me with questions, let me explain."

Jim crossed his arms. "Fine. Go."

Bree rubbed her face and took a deep breath. She explained

to him how Marion had showed up unannounced that morning and that she'd agreed to dinner to talk about things.

"Does Carson know she's here?"

"No. Nobody knows. Well, nobody knew. I know how it looks, really." Bree clasped her hands together over her chest. "I do. But what else was I supposed to do? She just showed up." Bree flailed her arms in frustration.

"So, what does she want?"

Bree sat on the low brick wall and put her face into her hands. "She wants me to come home. Well, not home. She wants me to go to San Diego." She looked up at Jim and watched the recognition sweep across his face.

"I wish I could say that it surprises me."

"Me, too." Bree doubted that Marion had thought twice about Bree's new life once she'd decided she wanted Bree back. It had always been that way. Even her decision to leave had been made without any consideration of how it would affect Bree. To say that Marion was motivated in life by complete selfishness was an understatement. The day Marion had left was as abrupt and unexpected as the day she'd returned, and the details held little personal sentiment or emotion.

"What did you tell her?"

Bree stood and looked at Jim. "Nothing. I even sat in the bathroom and questioned myself about it. This is what I've been waiting for, isn't it?"

"Yes. But when we stop wishing for the past and we open our hearts to the possibilities of a future, things happen that make us forget why we'd been waiting."

"And now she's back."

"Yes. But is that what you still want? What about your home and work and Carson? What are you going to tell her?"

"I don't know, Uncle Jim. I don't even know what to tell myself, or Marion."

"The truth, kiddo. You and Carson deserve the truth. Marion deserves nothing."

"I know. But what do I say? Oh, right." Bree waved her arms around with embellished indifference. "Hey, babe. So listen, Marion is back. We went to dinner, and she wants me to move to California with her. But don't worry, because I haven't decided what I'm doing yet."

"Bree, look at me. Carson is smart and kind. She knows your past, she knows what you've been through, and she isn't Marion. She doesn't deserve to be lied to and hurt the way that you were. And between you and me, I think you've already decided what you're going to do." Jim grabbed Bree's hands and squeezed them.

He was right; in her heart, she knew. "But is it the right decision?"

"I can tell you what I think, but you're the only one that knows the answer, sweetheart." Jim kissed her on the forehead. It was something he and Carson both did to make her feel better. As always, it worked. "Now, I better get back in there before Barbara decides to leave me here."

"Yeah, right." Bree knew that would never happen. Those two were made for each other, and now that Barbara had him, she wouldn't go anywhere without him.

Bree and Jim said their good-byes and returned to their own tables. Bree sat across from Marion and studied her. She looked good. If nothing else, she had taken great care of herself. "What are you really doing here, Marion?"

"I told you. I missed you. I want to be with you."

"That's it? You woke up yesterday and you suddenly missed me? It's been two and a half years, Marion." Bree needed more.

"Sort of. The last few months I've thought a lot about being alone, and I asked myself if there was one person I would bring here with me, who would it be? And of course, I thought of you. I knew you moved back here and didn't have any real ties. We have a few openings at the gallery, and I thought that if you came home to me and took a position, my life would be back to normal, just like it was in Boston."

Bree looked at Marion as if she had three heads. "You left me in Boston, Marion. You walked away from everything we built together and took a job on the other side of the country. Without me." Bree's ears burned. "Tell me this, were you cheating on me when you left?"

"What? Why would you ask that?" Marion shifted in her chair.

"Oh my God, you were. And you went to California with her, didn't you? What happened, Marion? Did she leave you? Or wait…You left her heartbroken in California waiting for you to come back?" Bree stood up from the table. "I can't believe you." Bree sat back down and lowered her voice. "No, I can. Because that's what you did to me. You left me alone and devastated to suffocate under the memories of our life together. And then you come here and offer me our life back because you figure I don't have anything better in mine?"

"Well, do you?" Marion leaned back in her seat and crossed her arms.

Bree stood up again. "Yes, I do. I have my family and my job, and I have Carson. This is my home now." She did have Carson, and Carson had her.

Marion stood and grabbed Bree's elbow. She pulled her close. "You're a silly little tour guide wasting your talent, intelligence, and education. I don't know or give a shit who this *Carson* is, but you don't need her because I'm here now. I'm your home, Bree."

Bree jerked her arm from Marion's grip. "I can't just pack up and leave the people I love as easily as you're able to. Good-bye, Marion." Bree picked up her purse and turned to leave.

"Wait. So is that a yes or no?"

Bree looked back and rolled her eyes before she turned away from Marion and left her standing alone at the table. She passed Barbara and Jim on her way out. She didn't stop, only forced a smile and left the restaurant.

Chapter Nineteen

Jim grabbed the mail from the interoffice box and flipped through the envelopes. He was headed to Carson's office, so he checked her mail slip and picked out the large FedEx package addressed to her. She had just taken off her gloves when he entered and set the large envelope on her desk. "For you."

Jim had no idea what it was although he'd read the label before he handed it over. He was curious to know what came addressed from the Dayton Art Institute in Ohio.

"Dayton?" Carson asked as she flipped the envelope around in her hands. She ripped open the seal and pulled out a thick folder.

"What is that?" Jim looked over her shoulder and picked up the empty envelope she'd set on the table. He repeated her earlier question. "Dayton?"

"Yeah," she responded as she opened the folder. "Oh."

"Oh what? What is it?" He peered over at the letter Carson read to herself. "Director of Preservation? Wow."

"It seems that I'm being recruited for a director position at the Dayton Art Institute. They want me to come out and meet with the board of directors in a couple weeks to see if I'd be interested in the job." Carson read the letter with a small hint of excitement. "Wow."

"That's amazing. I didn't even know you were interested in Dayton."

"I'm not. I mean, I wasn't. I'm not even sure how they got my name. This is wild." Carson set the envelope and its contents on her desk and stared at it.

"Wild indeed." Jim picked up the material and flipped through the pages. "What are you going to do? When do they want you?"

"I have no freaking idea. It says in a couple of weeks. So I don't have to decide right now. Besides, I don't even know if I want to move to Ohio."

"Right. Wow." Jim was dumbstruck.

"No kidding," Carson said. "Me, a director. It's unreal. It's not like I've never imagined myself as one. Hell, six months ago it was the only thing on my mind. I guess after thirteen years I just never expected it to be anywhere other than here at the Estate." Carson took the packet back from Jim and fingered the pages.

"This is an extraordinary opportunity. I'm sure they will allow you to think about it longer than two seconds. It's an enormous decision. Life changing." And Jim was concerned that it wasn't only Carson's life that it would change.

"It is. But you're right. I don't have to decide in two seconds. Although what would it hurt to go check it out? It's a free trip to Dayton and a little time off. I can't just turn them down without even hearing what they have to offer me." Carson smacked the papers in her hand and grinned.

Jim was discontented by the situation. It would have been out of character for her not to be intrigued by such an extraordinary opportunity. And although she was comfortable at the Biltmore, she had always kept herself very open when it came to her future. But he couldn't help but feel uneasy by the uncertainty of the prospect. It wasn't the offer that concerned him but the aftermath it could create, not only for him but more importantly for Bree. He was torn between supporting Carson and protecting Bree. "I know that you can't just let something like this pass you by. But please, just let Bree know."

"It's just an interview. There's nothing to tell her. If anything comes from the meeting I will certainly discuss it with her. But at this point it seems a little premature. No? Things are going great right here. Why would I want to change that?"

"Car, listen to me. I'm not telling you what to do. You are free to make your own decisions, but please don't keep her in the dark. I can't tell you how happy I am for you, and for Bree. And while I don't want this to be something you miss out on and end up regretting down the line, I also don't want you to break her heart in the process." The idea of watching Bree lose another person she loved twisted his heart. He squeezed her shoulder.

Carson looked at the envelope in front of her and then into his eyes. "Relax. It's just an interview, Jim."

"Just tell her. For me." He purposely avoided explaining his reasons to Carson as he had no intention of using guilt to discourage her from making her own decisions. After Jim left, he stopped in the hallway and stared back at the door. He prayed that Carson would do the right thing for both of his precious girls.

CHAPTER TWENTY

Carson showed Kelli around to the back of the house where everyone had gathered on the porch. She spotted Jim at the grill and raised her eyebrows in silent question. She didn't even have to speak, and he responded, "In the kitchen." She hadn't seen Bree in several days, and it was wearing on her ability to focus.

Carson slipped into the house through the dining room. She stopped and leaned against the jamb of the doorway of the kitchen and took the opportunity to rake her eyes over Bree. She might have been the most beautiful woman Carson had ever known. Carson loved nothing more than to gaze at her when she didn't know it. She watched as Bree stacked way too much onto the tray that she prepared to carry outside. With Bree's track record of mishaps, Carson knew that both she and the tray would never make it to the patio in one piece. She still adored the determined look on Bree's face as she lifted the tray and turned on her heel toward the doorway.

Bree took one step forward and gasped as the load swayed perilously. She paused mid-step and watched the stack until the movement stopped. She looked up and screamed at the unexpected sight of Carson leering from the doorway. As she lifted her arms in response, the tray tipped and everything began to fall forward. Carson lunged at the tumbling pile and caught the goods between her body and Bree's.

"Need some help?" Carson said as she pushed the items back and repositioned them onto the tray. Her heart raced and her stomach fluttered when Bree's eyes met hers.

Bree gave her a shy smile. "Hi."

"Hi." Carson blushed as she looked at Bree's sparkling eyes and pink lips. It seemed like forever since the last time she had felt Bree's soft, sensuous lips on hers. She missed it with her heart and soul, and she wished that the stupid tray or the awkwardness wasn't wedged between them.

Carson shifted the weight of the tray to herself. "I'll carry this."

"What? You don't think I can manage to get it out there in one piece?"

"No, babe. No, I don't." Carson loved when she could be there when Bree needed her. Even if it was for the small things, like carrying a dinner tray stacked with paper goods.

"Who am I kidding? You're right. Thank you."

Carson was glad to see Bree's face. She had thought about nothing but her for days, and she had ached to be apart from her. The more time Carson spent with Bree, the more she missed her when they were apart. She couldn't remember what had been more important in her life before Bree came into it, and Carson wasn't sure anything would ever be.

❖

When Jim had mentioned having a Sunday barbecue, Bree had no idea that he intended to follow through with it. Nevertheless, she was grateful for the happy distraction. Bree had little doubt of his intentions when he'd called up their closest friends and invited them that very morning, and she was surprised that everyone said yes. In spite of her anxiety over the conversation she needed to have with Carson, Bree was still very excited to see her.

Bree sat and watched her family and friends mix and mingle together. She'd had the last couple of days to let the reality of her decision about Marion sink in. There was a strange emptiness that had settled in her mind the moment she'd walked away from her, but it wasn't a void. It was a freedom. As she looked around at the ones she loved while they talked and laughed with ease, she believed it. Jim and Carson stood near the grill and sipped beer while they exerted their masculine dominance over the fire. When Jim put his arm around Carson, Bree's heart melted. It was a simple gesture, but one of love, and something Bree had never seen him do with anyone else. Bree couldn't help but smile as she rested her chin on her hands and admired the two people most dear in her life.

"She's a true heart, that one." Bree was so enchanted by them she hadn't noticed when Barbara sat next to her.

Without taking her eyes off them she responded, "They both are."

"So are you, you know."

Bree looked over at Barbara, who looked back at her with the love she'd only ever seen in her uncle's eyes. "Sometimes I wonder if I deserve it."

"Deserve what, sweetheart?" Barbara wrapped an arm around Bree's shoulders and pulled her in tightly.

"The way she looks at me." Since the day they'd met, Carson had looked at Bree like she was the most precious thing in the world.

"Everyone should be as lucky to be loved as much as she loves you. And you deserve what she has to give."

Bree looked at Barbara. "She loves me?"

"Since the first moment she saw you."

Bree looked back at them when she heard Carson laugh. "She loves me, for now. Because she doesn't know."

"You underestimate her, darling." Barbara waved when Jim and Carson looked over and smiled.

Bree smiled back. *She loves me.* "I truly hope you're right."

❖

Bree and Carson waved good-bye to Gwen and Suzanne before Bree closed Alan's car door and tapped on the roof. Carson slipped her hand into Bree's and was grateful when she didn't pull back. Since she had been standoffish most of the day, Carson had been reluctant to make any such move for fear that Bree would dismiss her. She was content to have Bree's hand in hers as they walked back around to the patio. Barbara tossed garbage into a bag while Kelli helped Jim put the cover on the grill.

Carson felt Bree squeeze her hand and pull her to a stop. Carson looked at Bree, who had an unexpected sadness on her face. "What's wrong? Are you feeling okay?"

"I need to talk to you." Bree had put it off as long as she could. She needed to get it over with, like ripping off a Band-Aid.

"Of course, babe." Carson's heart thumped in her chest and a lump rose into her throat.

Bree led her across the yard to the gazebo at the corner of the yard. They sat down side by side, and Bree turned herself to face Carson. "There's something I need to tell you. I'm not sure how to start or how to say it, but you deserve to know."

"God. I've never been so freaked out in all my life," Carson blurted out before she could even stop herself.

"I know. I'm so sorry about that." Bree grabbed Carson's hand and held it in both of hers. "Okay. I've been going over and over in my head the different ways to say this without it sounding worse than it is. But it always sounds the same. So, here it goes. Marion came back." Almost without breathing, Bree told Carson about Marion. "She showed up at my door like no time had passed and asked me to come home to San Diego. She wanted us to start over, to pick up where our lives left off."

Carson stood. She felt numb and dumbstruck. "Wow. Um, okay. I can't say that I was expecting anything you just said. My brain and heart are fighting between a thousand different questions." Carson looked down at the hand Bree squeezed mercilessly.

"I'm so sorry, Carson. Please listen, let me explain. I understand if you're mad that I didn't tell you before now. I just didn't know how or even what to tell you." Bree's voice cracked.

"I guess I only really have one question." Of course Carson had more than that, but she needed to know one above all the others. "What did you tell her?"

Bree looked up at Carson. "I…I didn't." Bree hadn't said anything to her. She had just walked out of the restaurant and never looked back.

Carson's throat tightened around the lump that she couldn't swallow. "You didn't? What do you mean you didn't?" Carson stood up, but Bree's shaking hand held fast to hers.

Bree refused to let her go. "Carson, wait. When she kissed me I felt nothing at all, nothing like I feel when you kiss me. I told her I had family here, and I had you. And then I said good-bye, and I left. It was so much more than she ever gave me when she walked away. She didn't deserve more than that."

"You kissed her?" The wind was thrust from her lungs as if she'd been hit by a truck.

"I did. Well, she kissed me." Tears welled up in Bree's eyes. "I was just so overwhelmed. She was there, standing in front of me like I'd dreamed for so long. But—"

Carson stood and grabbed the railing for support. She couldn't catch her breath even in the wide open air.

"Carson, please. For a very long time, Marion was my entire life. Long after she left, I wished for that moment. I never had any doubt about what I'd do when she came home. I'd fantasized about it a thousand times. She promised me, Carson. She's my wife. I told her I'd wait for her. But you—"

"Your what? You're still married?" Carson pulled her hand back and wrapped her arms around herself. She felt nauseous and light-headed.

Bree nodded and reached out for her, but Carson moved away, her heart breaking.

"You changed everything I ever thought I wanted." Bree closed her eyes and her tears fell freely.

"And what do you want, Bree? Because for the first time in my life I have no doubts or questions. I know what I want, and it's right here." Carson stepped forward and wiped the streak of tears from Bree's cheek. "And now you tell me that you aren't even free to be mine?"

"I am free, Carson. I told her that I couldn't just leave the people I care about the same way she did. Then I left. I left her standing there and I walked away. I chose you."

"But you're married, Bree. You can't just say it's over and that's that." No matter how much she wished it was, it was not that simple.

"I know. But it is. I have the papers. I'll sign them right now." Bree stood.

The knot in Carson's throat tightened again. "They're not even signed? I know you've been scared and confused lately, but I never put less than a hundred percent into whatever this is or was. No matter how uncertain I was about what I was doing. It wasn't even something I knew I wanted until I met you. I lo…I've got to go."

Bree's eyes opened in surprise. "I…you…what?"

"I love you."

"Oh, Carson, I—"

Carson didn't know what Bree was going to say, but she wasn't ready to hear whatever it was. "Don't."

Bree stepped back in surprise. "What?"

Carson stepped forward. "Please don't say whatever it is you were about to say. I've never done this before so I'm not sure how it's supposed to be, but I'm almost certain this isn't it. Not like this, Bree. I need to go."

"Carson."

She kissed Bree on the lips and excused herself. As Carson left Bree standing alone in the gazebo, she struggled to contain the burning tears that blinded her. She hoped with everything she had that it wasn't good-bye, but as she walked away from Bree, she steeled herself for the possibility that it was.

CHAPTER TWENTY-ONE

Carson and Kelli drove back to the warehouse in near silence. The exceptions being the halfhearted attempts that Kelli made to get Carson's attention. Carson replayed the words in her mind. *She's my wife.* The idea of Bree kissing another woman made her sick to her stomach, but the fact that she and Marion were still married ripped into her chest. Why had Bree kept that from her? What was the point? *If she loved me, why didn't she sign the papers? Why hasn't she just been honest with me? Would she have told me that she loves me, too?* While Carson's head wasn't certain, something inside her soul told her yes. "What am I doing?"

"What are you talking about?" Kelli was surprised by Carson's outburst but encouraged the conversation.

Carson kept her eyes on the road ahead. "With Bree. What am I doing?"

"I don't understand what you're asking, Car." Kelli adjusted herself in the seat so that she had turned her body to face Carson. "What happened?"

Carson gave Kelli the watered-down version of what Bree had told her just twenty minutes earlier and exposed the painful truth of the situation. "And then I left."

"Wow. Okay. Let's think about this."

"What is there to think about? She's still married."

Kelli rolled her eyes. "When has a ring ever discouraged you from getting what you want?"

"This is a little different than that." Carson wondered if it really was different. In this case she knew that Bree was no longer with Marion and she had been honest with her about her feelings, if not the specifics. "No, it's very different. I wanted this one to work out. For the first time, I wasn't afraid of the possibility that this could be something."

"So, let's recap. Bree's ex showed up unannounced at her door, asked her to come home, and Bree responded by walking out on her. Yes? Is that about the gist of it?"

"Well, you forgot the part where Bree jumped into her arms and kissed her. But yes, basically."

"Right. So she told you that she kissed her, then walked out on her. And she offered to sign the papers in front of you to prove it?"

"Yes." *She chose me.*

"Why do you think she told you all of that? I mean really? If she was going to take her ex-wife back and move away, wouldn't she have just said that instead of telling you every detail?"

Carson had never imagined that she would find someone she cared for as much as she did Bree. She had never wanted to. Yet there she was, hoping that Bree meant what she said, while the thought of losing her scared Carson beyond words. If tomorrow Bree decided to go back to Marion it would kill her, but she would not regret the days and moments that she'd spent with Bree. "I'd do anything for her, but how do I just let her go?"

"If she wanted to go, she'd already be gone, Carson."

While they were at a traffic light, Carson's phone vibrated and she reached into her front pocket to grab it. She held her breath as her heart raced. She took a deep breath before she looked at the screen.

I need you to come away with me this weekend. Please. -B

"I take it by the smile on your face that it wasn't a text telling you she was moving to San Diego?" Kelli smiled as she turned to face forward.

Carson read it to herself ten times more before she read it aloud to Kelli.

"Yes. Say yes!" Kelli reached out for Carson's phone. "Give it to me. I'll say yes."

Carson pulled her phone against her chest. "I can do it." There was no other answer that Carson would've given except for yes. Carson took a deep breath and replied.

I can think of nothing else I'd rather do -C.

I'm sorry. I miss you. XOXO -B

Carson's stomach filled with butterflies. She couldn't have been happier to know that Bree was not only thinking about her but that she missed her.

I miss you, too, sweetheart. See you soon. -C

❖

"So, how are things going between you and Barbara? Huh, stud muffin?" Carson slugged Jim in the arm and made exaggerated winking faces at him.

"You know, I don't think I approve of my daughter dating someone so…immature."

Carson's mouth dropped open and then clapped shut. "Fine, then we will run away together, like Romeo and Juliet."

"Uh, you do realize that they both die in that story, right?"

"Oh, right. Hey, this isn't about me. This is about you and your lovely lady. How are things?"

"It's great, Car. She's an amazing woman. I think about

her every moment we're apart. She's funny and smart and I can't believe I've waited so long to take this step. And damn is she sexy."

"Have you…" Carson made with the winks again.

"Stop that. No, we haven't. And you know, I'm not asking you the same question because I know your answer is also no."

"But—"

"No. The answer you tell your girlfriend's father is always no, right?"

"Right. No." Carson laughed, but she knew he was dead serious. They talked about everything, but sex with his daughter was not one of those things, and she was okay with that.

"So, besides that, how are things with the two of you?" Carson started to smile. "Have you told her about the interview in Dayton yet?"

Carson's smiled vanished. "Nah, not yet. We just made it through the Marion thing and it's just not the first thing on my mind each time I see her."

"Don't you think—"

She cut him off before he could finish. "Jim, she makes me so happy. I can see tomorrow when I look at her. I want to wake up every day and be the reason she smiles." Carson felt it to her core. When she listened to Bree describe her dream wedding, she saw herself by her side promising forever. "I want to keep her safe and protect her but also encourage and support her. She deserves so much, and I want to give her everything she needs."

"When is your interview?"

"Next week. I'll talk to her after this weekend." Carson knew in her heart that she didn't want the job in Dayton. She also knew that Jim wanted her to be certain in her head as well. In the end, it was his duty as a father to protect Bree from heartache and pain. Carson loved her life in Asheville, and she had met someone she could share that life with, but he was right about making sure that she had no regrets. She had to be sure that she could offer Bree everything she deserved.

"Sooner is better than later."

She agreed for the most part, but it just wasn't the big deal that Jim was making it out to be. There was no sense in getting Bree worked up over something that was probably not going to matter in two weeks. And in the end, it was a decision only she had to make.

CHAPTER TWENTY-TWO

Carson arrived at Bree's house. As always, Bree felt her presence before she saw her. She looked out the window and watched Carson make her way up the steps of the front porch. Their eyes met, and Bree's heart leapt. She knew there wasn't another place in the world that she wanted to be at that moment except in Carson's arms. Bree tried to wait until Carson had at least rung the doorbell, but her feet refused. She flung the door open and they stood within inches of each other and simultaneously said, "Hi."

Bree giggled as she twisted her hands in front of her. "How are you?"

"Better, now."

"Me, too. Are you ready to go?"

"Absolutely."

Bree pressed the button on her remote and popped the trunk of her car. She reached inside the door for her bags, but Carson beat her to it. They both gripped the handle of Bree's luggage and smiled as their shoulders bumped. Bree stared into Carson's deep, soulful eyes. Her body trembled with excitement and anticipation of the days, and nights, ahead. She didn't know who made the first move, all she knew was the feeling of serenity that swelled within her as their lips met.

They loaded the bags into the car. Instead of reaching up to close the trunk, Bree moved in to wrap her arms around Carson. Before either of them realized what was happening a bouquet of flowers was stuffed between them. "What the hell?"

"Hey, babe. Surprise." Marion grinned wryly as she wedged herself in with the flowers. Bree and Carson had little choice but to step back from each other.

Bree looked at Carson, whose face burned brighter with each second that passed. Bree knew that Carson didn't know who Marion was or what she looked like, but the recognition on her face was unmistakable. "Um, Marion, what are you doing here?"

"Surprising you. Obviously." She waved the bouquet up and down without any regard to the fact that she brushed it against Carson's shirt.

Bree circled around Marion and the offending bouquet until she was at Carson's side. "Marion. This is Carson. Carson, Marion." Carson held out her hand for a polite shake into which Marion put the flowers.

"Seriously, Marion?" Bree took the flowers out of Carson's hand and slapped them back onto Marion's chest.

"What?" Marion smirked.

"What are you doing here?" Bree asked again.

"Fine. I'm here to…" Marion paused and looked at Carson. She waited for her to take the cue to leave, but Carson didn't move. "Maybe we could go somewhere else?"

"Here works for me."

Marion looked at Carson. "She always did prefer grand gestures." Carson rolled her eyes. "I want you to come home, Bree. I want you to get a real job and stop wasting time in this place." She gestured all around, making sure to include Carson.

Carson stepped back, but Bree grabbed her arm and held on. "No, Marion. I told you. This is where I belong."

Marion scoffed. "You can't be serious. You would give up our life together to stay here?" Marion looked at Carson.

"No, Marion. You gave up our life together, two and a half years ago."

"I was planning our future. Building my career in order to—"

Bree held up her free hand, refusing to let Carson go. "Stop! Give me a break, Marion. You were planning *your* future, building *your* career and *your* success. Your choices had nothing to do with me. They never did. You came back because somehow I fit into your life again. But I have my own life now, and I don't need you or yours."

"She'll never give you what I can." Marion pointed at Carson without even looking at her.

"She won't. You're right. But I've had enough heartbreak in my life, so I'm okay with that. Um, I'd move my finger unless you want her to break it off."

Carson smiled as Marion dropped her hand.

"You're my wife, Bree. Remember?"

Bree's stomach dropped, and she released Carson's hand. She left both women standing in silence, hanging on those words as she leaned into the car. Bree returned with a large yellow envelope and held it out to Marion. "Not anymore. Those are your copies. I was going to mail them out to you on our way out of town today, but this is better."

Marion opened the stamped envelope and slipped out the papers. She nodded but said nothing as she slid them back. She cleared her throat and said, "I see. So that's it."

"Yes, Marion. That's it." She took Carson's hand in hers and squeezed it. "*We* really need to get on the road. The freeway is that way"—Bree pointed—"not that you ever had a problem finding it."

❖

Bree zipped through the switchbacks along the Blue Ridge Parkway. There had been a couple of times when she looked over and saw Carson's white-knuckle grip on the handle of the door. To save Carson's sanity, Bree eased off the throttle and relaxed into a scenic, Sunday drive pace. She was glad she did, as there was no reason they needed to be in any sort of hurry. Plus, she wanted to make every moment with Carson last as long as possible. They stopped at one of the many overlooks that dotted the parkway as it wound higher into the Smoky Mountains.

That morning, while she waited for Carson to arrive at her house, she sat on the couch in silent thought. It was something she did a lot of. It wasn't even that she would think of something significant or important but rather random thoughts, ideas, or even memories. She, without a doubt, had a very active mind. Bree hadn't told Carson what she had planned, because until that morning she herself had no idea. She'd made reservations for a cabin, but otherwise she'd decided to wing it.

Bree recalled the night of her birthday dinner and the moments she had shared with Carson on the mountain road. Bree felt that it was a special part of Carson's own self that she had gifted to her. It wasn't a tangible one, but it was worth more than anything Bree had ever gotten. Then the idea hit her. She would take Carson to someplace that was a part of her. Someplace that had helped her through the roughest parts of her life.

According to the informational sign, it was possible to

see for ten miles, depending on the weather and cloud cover. Bree knew how moody Mother Nature could be when you got into her territory. So she had been happy to see the low-level clouds in the distance. It was the sort of day she had hoped for. Bree and Carson sat in the plush grass on the edge of a bluff that dropped into a forested ravine. The beautiful mountains in the distance provided an awe-inspiring beginning to their weekend together. They sat for several minutes in silence as they took in their vast surroundings. It was Carson's welcome voice that broke the stillness. "I don't think I've ever felt such an overwhelming sense of peace."

"I remember the first time Uncle Jim brought me up here. It wasn't long after we'd begun our new life as a family. He'd watched me so many times as I lay in the yard and stared at the sky for hours on end. One day he stretched out in the grass beside me and asked what I was looking at. 'The clouds,' I told him."

Bree stared out into the distance as she recalled the beginning of her connection with the clouds. Carson stroked her hair, and a swirling sense of contentment covered her.

"He asked if I was looking for animals, but I wasn't. I was looking for my mom and dad. I wanted to…I needed to ask them so many questions. I wasn't raised in a religious home, so I had very little knowledge of what heaven was. I just knew it was in the sky somewhere. I remember thinking that they were the clouds. Like, somehow when they died, they had become them." Tears filled Bree's eyes as she told Carson her most private memories. "I wished every moment for one more chance to hug them."

"Oh God, Bree. I am so sorry. I wish I had been there to hold you and comfort you through that." Carson wrapped her arms around Bree and pulled her in close against her.

Bree had never felt as safe as she did with Carson holding

her. "I still can't remember anything Jim might have said after that. I don't imagine that he did. All I remember after that was the day he took me for a drive up to Mt. Mitchell to touch the clouds. From that day forward, it became my place of comfort. It's the place I go when I need peace in my mind or my life. It's my happy place. I can stand in the clouds and let them embrace me. I can ask my questions and release my fears as they envelop me." Bree looked into Carson's eyes. "I need and want very much to share this with you, Carson."

"I have never wanted anything more in my life." Carson stroked the remaining tears from Bree's face and kissed her lips.

❖

When Bree pulled into a parking spot at their destination, Carson became very excited. While she loved Bree's car, she didn't love Bree driving the car. She jumped out of the vehicle and kissed the earth like a sailor after a yearlong voyage. Carson hoped Bree planned to spend a little while on solid ground before they headed back down the mountain. "Wow, look at that." Carson pointed to the overlook at the edge of the mountain as the clouds swooped up and swirled over the ridge.

Bree smiled. "I know. Come on." Bree grabbed Carson's hand and led her closer.

They stopped at a short stone wall that faced the wind as it brought the cool, damp clouds rushing up the side of the mountain. Bree told the story of why this spot was the one place in the world she could let everything go. Bree stepped forward, held her arms out to her sides, and closed her eyes. Carson watched the clouds swirl around Bree, blowing her hair wildly in the wind. Bree's power over nature was almost mystical. Carson was mesmerized by her magic. She stood back and let Bree have the time she needed. She knew right then that she would wait forever if Bree asked her to.

After a few more moments, Bree turned back to Carson and held out her hand toward her. Carson took it and allowed herself to be wrapped around Bree's body. "I want to be with you," Bree said. "I'm ready to let go of all of the fear and anger and move on with my life. With you." Carson could feel the freedom and release as the mist lifted the negativity from her and carried it away into the sky.

Carson moved around in front of Bree, and her heart raced. "I want that, too. So very much." Carson kissed Bree with unbridled desire. It was a kiss so strong and passionate that Bree would never mistake just how much she was wanted and needed. Carson had never been so blessed by anyone in her life. Carson held Bree's face in her hands and looked into her eyes. "You are amazing. I want to do everything I can to make you happy. Anything."

Bree smiled. "You already do."

She chose me. Carson wanted to scream from the rooftops that the woman she loved chose to be with her.

❖

Bree let Carson drive back down the mountain. It was clear from her earlier verdigris complexion that Carson did not enjoy Bree's driving. Bree couldn't blame her. She never denied being a terrible driver and sometimes surprised herself when she made it to her destination. Plus, Bree liked how sexy and confident Carson looked as she drove the Nissan, so it was a win-win.

CHAPTER TWENTY-THREE

The cabins Bree chose were at the edge of the state park. She had stayed in them a handful of times in her youth and always remembered them with such fondness. It was a no-brainer as to where they would stay for the night. The authentic log cabins were built in the early 1900s, restored, and furnished with period antiques. It would be a shame not to share them with someone who loved history as much as Carson did. It wasn't until they pulled onto the property that she remembered the quaint little restaurant and became famished. Before she could stop herself, she mumbled, "Food."

Carson laughed. "Thank God I'm not the only one."

"No, you aren't. I'm starving. We can go there first or check in first, either way is fine."

Carson opted to eat first, and Bree was more than okay with it.

After they ate, they checked in at the main lodge and headed to their cabin. The "Snuggle In" was distinguished from the other cabins by the hand-carved sign that hung over the doorway.

Once inside, Bree and Carson put their bags down and checked things out. It was just as Bree remembered it from her childhood, rustic and charming without a hint of extravagance. She was also pleased with the quality of the furniture selections and restorations. She assumed that Carson would make the same curious inspections, yet she didn't. Carson sat in a chair and flipped through one of the local guidebooks she'd picked up from the side table. "Whatcha lookin' at?" Bree said as she sauntered over to where Carson sat.

"It's a local guide for Western North Carolina." Carson held up the book so Bree could see the cover.

"Aha, anything interesting?"

"Um, yeah. Did you know there is a zip line course out in Bryson? I didn't know that. Oh, and look, the train. I did that once a few years back." Carson flipped through the magazine. She turned page after page without stopping to read a single one.

"Carson?" Bree thought she would've been the nervous one. She never would have expected Carson to play that part.

Carson looked up. She still turned the pages without even looking. "Yeah?"

Bree reached for the book. "You have no idea what you are even looking at, do you?"

Carson let her slip the book from her hands as she stared up at Bree. "Not the faintest."

Without even looking, Bree tossed the book in the direction of the desk. She straddled Carson in the chair without ever taking her eyes off her. When she heard the book land where she intended, she was surprised that she had pulled it off. Until of course it flipped off the edge and fell with a crash into the trash can. "Well, it was almost sexy."

"Trust me, it's still pretty damn sexy." Carson ran her finger along the top of Bree's thigh.

Bree slid her hand up Carson's arm to her shoulder and ran her finger up the side of Carson's neck and around her ear. Carson tilted her head to the side and Bree replaced her wandering finger with her tongue. She nibbled her way back down the sensitive skin of Carson's neck while her hands teased and pulled at the hem of Carson's shirt. She exposed a hint of soft skin, and Bree slid her fingertips back and forth inside the waistband of Carson's jeans. Carson's muscles twitched at the touch, and the reaction fueled Bree's need.

The teasing made Carson groan, and the sound blazed through her. Bree touched Carson's parted lips. She'd had so many dreams about those lips and all the things she wanted them to do to her. Bree licked her lips before she kissed Carson's bottom one and sucked on it.

❖

Carson's need throbbed as Bree nipped and sucked on her skin. She could feel the heat between Bree's legs as she pressed herself onto Carson's thigh. She was wet, and she had no doubt that Bree was, too. As she thought about how Bree would feel in her hand, Carson realized she was losing her control. She needed her, to touch her and taste her. Carson twisted her fingers into Bree's wild hair and pulled her close. Feverishly, she claimed Bree's mouth. Bree's response was instant as she opened her mouth and let Carson's tongue tangle with her own. When Bree moaned, Carson's desire raged and all control she had was lost.

She grasped the hem of Bree's shirt and lifted it over her head and tossed it to the floor. Carson ran her hands over Bree's bare shoulders and kissed the smooth skin. She traced her fingers down along the straps of Bree's black lace bra and continued along the curve of her full breasts. Carson watched as Bree's nipples tightened through the delicate fabric. Carson lost all control. She gripped Bree's waist and stood. Bree gasped and wrapped her arms and legs around Carson. In two long strides, she reached the bed and lowered Bree down onto her back.

Carson stood at the edge and allowed her eyes to roam over Bree's beautiful body. She tugged her shirt over her head in one smooth motion and dropped it to the floor. Her eyes locked on Bree's as she released the snap and zipper of her jeans. Before she pushed them down, Bree sat up and reached for the loose waistband and pulled Carson down over her. "I want you, Carson Harper. Please touch me," Bree begged.

"Anything." Carson circled the hard nipple that pressed against the lace before she leaned down and sucked on it through the fabric. Bree arched her back and pushed herself into Carson's mouth. It wasn't enough. Carson tugged the material down and released a full perfect breast with a hard, rosy nipple. She flicked her tongue over the tip before she took it into her mouth. Bree whimpered.

Carson felt Bree lift her knee and press her thigh between Carson's legs. Carson rubbed herself against Bree's leg, which fueled her need with every thrust. Carson pushed herself back onto her knees. "I need to feel you against me." Carson flicked the button on Bree's pants and pulled them off as Bree released her bra. Carson lowered herself onto Bree. Every inch of skin that connected between them surged with electricity. Bree spread her legs and Carson slid herself against Bree's wetness.

Bree ran her hands down Carson's back and squeezed her ass and pulled her tight against her. Carson pressed herself into Bree before she pulled back and slipped her fingers between them. She slid through the wet folds and coated her hand with Bree's slick desire. She eased inside, and Bree gasped. "Oh, God…" Bree bucked her hips against Carson's thrusting hand.

Carson pushed her fingers deeper. Bree wrapped her legs around Carson's hips and her hands gripped the sheets. She was close, and Carson could feel it as Bree tightened around her hand. "Come for me, baby."

"Yes. I'm going to."

As Bree pulsed against her fingers, Carson felt herself throb. She was as close as Bree was and without even a single touch from her. Carson had never before experienced such a deep connection with a lover. She had never felt so joined in pleasure. As Bree's body stiffened, Carson removed her hand and pressed her swollen center against Bree's. They both cried out at the spark of pleasure that jolted through them in that instant. Bree wrapped her arms around Carson as she collapsed over her and closed her eyes. Their hearts pounded in their chests as they both struggled to catch their breath.

Bree chuckled, and Carson looked at her through a sated fog. "Oh my, that laugh sounded almost devilish."

"Maybe it was." Bree smiled mischievously before she scooted down and out from under Carson's body.

"Where are you going?" Carson asked as she raised her eyebrows.

Bree slipped toward the end of the bed and down the length of Carson's body until she reached her destination. She pushed Carson over her and grabbed the hips that now hovered above her. Carson took a deep breath of anticipation right before she felt Bree's warm breath between her legs. Carson's legs shook and she prayed that she was able to hold herself up. She grabbed the top of the headboard for support just as Bree pulled her down to her mouth. Carson gasped at the contact. Bree's tongue slipped through her velvet folds and flicked her swollen clit. Her body jerked in response. When Bree slipped her fingers inside and sucked on Carson's pulsing tip, she cried out. She reached back to touch Bree, but her body writhed in pleasure beyond her control. Her body shuddered and tightened into a single knot of bliss. "Oh shit."

Bree slipped out from beneath her just as Carson crumpled to her back in a heap of exhaustion and satisfaction. Bree kissed her way inch by delicious inch up Carson's slick body and wrapped her arms and legs around her. Bree laid her head on Carson's chest and listened as the pounding rhythm slowed to a steady beat until they were both fast asleep.

Chapter Twenty-four

From the moment they returned from their weekend away, Carson had been inundated with work. Most nights she hadn't gotten out of the building until close to midnight, which meant she and Bree had seen very little of each other, the few exceptions being the moments they were able to sneak off into a stairwell or vacant room.

"Have I ever told you how much I enjoy doing this?" Carson kissed Bree's neck. "And this," she said when she got to her ear.

Bree knew how much, but she wanted to hear Carson say it. She tilted her head and offered more skin for Carson to do with as she wished. "No, how much?"

Carson groaned and pulled Bree in tight against her body. "So much that I wish we didn't have clothes on right now."

"Believe me, having you naked on top of me has been all I've been able to think about all week."

Carson grunted and slumped onto Bree's shoulder. "Oh God. Not helping, babe."

"Oh no? So sorry about that." Bree ran her hands down the length of Carson's back and into her back pockets, giving a gentle squeeze.

Carson groaned. "Sorry? Really? Just for that..." With

Bree's hands deep in her pockets, Carson took advantage of her restriction and untucked Bree's shirt in one swift pull. Bree sucked a breath in through her teeth as Carson slipped her hand underneath her shirt and cupped her breast before she lightly pinched her nipple through the fabric.

"Oh my, mmm." Bree closed her eyes and licked her lips. Carson pushed Bree back against the wall and pressed her thigh between Bree's legs. A loud slam boomed from the landing above. "Shit." Bree pushed Carson backward and fumbled with her shirt. As she thrashed and whirled, Carson leaned back and watched Bree struggle to compose herself. Bree's heart pounded in her ears.

Carson chuckled, and Bree looked up at her. She raised an eyebrow and peered up the steps to the floor above. There was no one coming. "What? Who...What was that?"

Carson snickered. "It's your uncle. I told him where I would be and to come get us in ten minutes."

"Are you freaking kidding me?" Bree swatted at Carson. "That nearly gave me a damn heart attack."

Carson pulled Bree to her amorously. "Don't worry. I know CPR." Carson winked before she placed a soft kiss on Bree's lips. "Let's go. It's lunchtime." Carson entwined her fingers with Bree's and led her up the stairs.

Bree followed behind Carson. She couldn't help but stare at the perfect way Carson's jeans fit her. Bree let herself imagine all the different ways she would get them off. She wanted Carson in every way possible, and if she didn't get more of her soon, she was going to go crazy. "Damn."

"What?"

Bree looked up. Carson held open the door but blocked Bree from passing. "Did you just say 'damn'?"

"I, uh, no." Bree's face blushed red. "That wasn't supposed to be out loud."

"But I like it." Carson tugged Bree's arm toward her. She gave her a quick peck before heading into the room.

Jim and Barbara stood at the opposite side of the large room. To anyone else they appeared to be nothing more than two innocent people observing and discussing the details of the restoration work being done. However, it was clear to Bree that the two lovebirds were oblivious of everything except each other. Bree wondered if it was how she and Carson looked when they were in a room together. She hoped so. "Hey, guys."

"Hi," Barbara said. She was in a delightful mood, and it looked wonderful on her.

"Ready for lunch?" Jim asked as he wrapped his arm around Bree's shoulders and pulled her close.

"Ready when you are."

The four of them walked into the hall and out toward the conservatory. Jim and Carson's cadence synced up in the lead as Bree and Barbara chitchatted and followed along behind. The sudden silence of the ladies caused Jim and Carson to stop and turn around. Bree and Barbara had halted at the edge of the terrace and looked back toward the front lawn. They backtracked their steps to see what had the women so mesmerized. Neither Jim nor Carson said a word as they witnessed Bree's and Barbara's whimpers and sighs over the wedding being conducted below.

"Oh. It's so beautiful. I remember when I was a little girl how I'd love to come out here and watch the weddings on the lawn," Bree reminisced.

"I remember the first time I saw a wedding here, I thought 'That's it. That's my dream wedding,'" Barbara said.

"I know. I don't think I've ever had any other idea or fantasy about where I'd get married. Oh. Look at her dress." Bree and Barbara sighed in unison while Jim and Carson glanced at each other with wide eyes.

"My favorites were the ones over there." Bree pointed in the direction of the wisteria arbors. "In the spring when the wisteria blooms, with the spirals of rose petals on the grass down the aisle. Oh, could you imagine?" Bree's voice was wistful as she laid her head on Barbara's shoulder.

"One day, my dear," Barbara whispered as she took Bree's hand in hers and patted it.

Jim and Carson cleared their throats and brought Bree and Barbara out of their joint daydream. They turned around as Carson and Jim kicked the ground and shuffled. Both of them had their hands clasped at their backs, and Bree laughed at their childish mannerisms. "Very subtle. Come on, Barbara. The boys are bored and hungry." Bree linked her arm with Carson's and headed off toward the café.

Chapter Twenty-five

Carson hunched over her desk and stared at the revised restoration schedule. With her headphones in she couldn't hear a thing around her, and that included whoever had come up behind her to cup their hands over her eyes. Carson shrieked and ripped her ear buds out of her head. "What the f—"

"Guess who?" a woman's voice whispered as she pressed her weight into Carson's back to keep her from turning around.

"Well, anyone daring enough to sneak up on me better be prepared for the consequences, no matter who they are." Carson hated being scared or startled, and everyone knew it. Carson brushed her fingers over the hands that still covered her eyes.

"And what would the punishment be for my actions?" she whispered to Carson before running her tongue along her ear.

"Oh, it's changing by the second."

"Well, that's not exactly a compelling reason not to do it, now is it?" the woman said before she kissed the nape of Carson's neck.

Carson enjoyed every bit of the unexpected seduction. It was a new move for Bree, and Carson took great pleasure in it. Carson grabbed the hands and pulled them down in front of her and held them still as her eyes adjusted to the light. When her vision cleared, she looked at the hands she held. She would recognize those beautiful hands anywhere. She spun around in her chair and looked at Bree. Bree's eyes were dark with lust, and it sent a shiver through Carson's body. "Dammit, Bree, you take my breath away every time I look at you."

Bree leaned in. She hung just a breath away from Carson's lips and whispered, "I'll give you all of mine in return." Bree's kiss sealed the promise.

Carson's heart fluttered and her soul melted. Everything she had was Bree's. There was no doubt.

Bree's arms rested over Carson's shoulders as she wedged her hips between Carson's legs. "Tell me you don't have to work late tonight."

"Well, I…"

"Pleeeease?"

Carson's stomach flipped hearing Bree almost beg. "No, sweetheart. I'm not working late tonight. I was just finishing things up when you interrupted me with this visit." Carson slipped her hands into the back pockets of Bree's slacks.

"Yay. So, do you want to stay with me tonight? We can make dinner, watch a movie, or we could just go to bed." Bree winked. She slipped her fingers between the buttons of Carson's shirt and stroked the underside of her breast.

"Mmm, yes, but I can't guarantee that we'll make it to your bed. Hell, baby, if you don't stop that we won't even make it out of this office."

She pinched Carson's nipple, drawing a sharp hiss. She kept the tightened nipple between her fingers. "Again, I'm not seeing the compelling reason."

When Bree twisted a little harder and bit her bottom lip, Carson gripped Bree's hands in hers. She was two seconds away from taking Bree right there on the desk in her office if Carson didn't restrain herself and Bree's wandering hands.

"Give me thirty minutes. You can ride with me to my place so I can get some clothes and such. Then we can head over to your place, okay?"

Bree looked at her imprisoned hands and made a childlike frown before she looked up and smiled widely. "I think that's a wonderful idea. I can't wait to see your place, from the inside, of course. Not from the flat of my back on the sidewalk." Bree laughed out loud.

Carson laughed and then feigned seriousness. "Funny."

Bree still chuckled. "Okay, babe. You finish your stuff and I'll meet you in the parking lot in a little bit." She gave Carson a quick peck and left.

"Yep. I'm officially hopeless." Carson grinned and turned around to finish her work.

❖

Bree walked to the staff parking lot with Jim and Barbara to wait for Carson. Bree was excited to see that Carson had ridden her bike to work that day. She hadn't been on it since their first date to Lake Lure. Just when she thought she couldn't be any more excited she spotted Carson, and her heart skipped. Carson had on her tailored leather jacket and a pair of snug-fitting jeans. Bree was transfixed by her cool blue eyes. *Damn, she's hot.*

"Hey, babe," Carson said when she stopped in front of Bree.

"Uh, I, um…hi." She couldn't have made a complete word if her life had depended on it. She welcomed the kiss that saved her from any further embarrassment.

"Ready?" Carson asked as she walked toward her bike.

Again, real words eluded Bree, so she just nodded. She heard Jim and Barbara laugh. She shot them a look and stuck out her tongue. It was a childish gesture, but as long as Carson didn't see it she didn't care. To make sure she hadn't seen, she looked over where Carson stood next to her bike and winked back at her. "Oh. For goodness sake." Bree's cheeks set fire, and she wanted to bury herself right there in the dirt.

"Babe. Get over here, and get on the bike."

Bree gave Jim a quick hug before she mounted the bike behind Carson. "Dinner and a movie tonight, right?" Jim and Barbara both nodded. Bree slipped on her helmet and wrapped her arms around Carson before they rumbled out of the parking lot.

❖

It hadn't taken more than five minutes to get from the lot to Carson's building in the arts district. Carson pulled onto the sidewalk and then into the large bay that was open to the street. She parked off to the side and cut the engine. She slid off first and then helped Bree. Bree looked around at the enormous stone blocks scattered about the room in their various stages of completion. She admired anyone who had such a wonderful talent and gift.

Carson weaved through the maze of sculptures toward the back of the warehouse. "Kelli should be here somewhere," she said.

A fire-red-haired woman appeared from behind a boulder. She stared down at the hand she had shoved into the neckline of her low-cut tank top. "I'm here. Ouch."

"What the hell are you doing?" Carson asked while they watched Kelli fondle her left breast.

"I'm putting Vaseline on my nipples," she said nonchalantly. Kelli was focused on her chest and still hadn't looked up. She plucked open the other side of her shirt and shifted her hand and attention to the other breast. She grimaced and whimpered in pain.

"Uh, why in the world are you doing that?" Carson asked, and Bree was so glad she had. She found that she both wanted and needed to know with a disturbing curiosity.

"Kim was way rough with my nips last night, so they're a little raw. I can't wear a bra because it rubs like a bitch. And the Vaseline seems to help with the tenderness."

Bree was surprised but pleased to know that new tidbit of information. "Good to know."

Kelli looked up as she adjusted her freshly moistened nipple and squeaked. "Oh shit, Bree! How are you?" Kelli held out her hand for Bree's. They all looked at Kelli's greasy hand before she withdrew her offer and smiled. "If it was just Carson here I'd wipe this on her shirt. But I'll behave," she said as she wiped the residue onto her own shorts instead.

They all laughed. "Thanks for that," Carson said. "We're here to pick up a couple of things. I'm staying at Bree's tonight, and I need my piggy pajamas."

Kelli made a disgusted face. "You better be kidding. Those things are hideous."

"You really do have piggy pajamas?" Bree didn't think Carson could be cuter than she was at that moment.

Carson blushed and looked back and forth between them. "Yes, I do, and no, they aren't."

Kelli and Bree both cooed and giggled at Carson. "Aww…"

"Oh no. This is not happening." Carson grabbed Bree's hand and pulled her to the staircase.

"But I want to talk more about your jammies…" Bree chortled as she stumbled behind Carson as she reached out for Kelli.

"Nope. Not happening."

"Call me. We'll talk." Kelli hollered after them as they climbed the steps.

Bree was impressed by Carson's apartment. Of course, from what she knew of Carson's work, she was correct in her assumption that it would be both pristine and tasteful. She had a fine eye for decorating. It was a large industrial and lofty space. Bree guessed that it was once a well-used office space for a large manufacturing warehouse below. Carson had the space filled with beautiful antiques and exceptional historic restorations. It was a wonderful combination of old and new, and it was 100 percent Carson. It was a space that anyone would be out of their mind not to fall in love with.

"Make yourself at home. I'll just be a minute." Carson kissed Bree on the forehead and disappeared down the hallway.

"Take your time." Bree explored the space and its furniture and artwork. She was in heaven. The west-facing wall of the large open great room was made entirely of glass and wood. Each six-foot section of crystal-clear pane glass was separated by a sixteen-foot-tall, hand-hewn barn wood beam. Bree stroked the beautiful wood worn and aged from time. The massive beams still contained the original tenon and mortise joints used during construction. A flash of light caught her eye, and she noticed the river below as the setting sun glinted off its surface.

Bree heard Carson come up behind her but didn't turn around. Carson slipped her arms around her waist and rested her chin on Bree's shoulder. "Ready when you are, sweetheart."

"This place is amazing, Carson. And this…" Bree touched the wooden divider again.

"A-hundred-and-fifty-year-old white oak timbers. They were given to me years ago by a good friend of mine, a vintage timber collector. I had them for a long time before I knew what

I was going to do with them. When I bought this place I had somewhere to put everything I love and worked so hard on."

Bree turned around in Carson's arms. "Amazing. Just like you."

"You haven't seen the rest of it. Come." Carson clasped Bree's hand and led her on a tour of the apartment.

Every room was furnished with the same precision and distinctiveness as the living room, but it was the master bedroom that took Bree's breath away. The bedroom was a vast space with the same floor-to-ceiling glass and timber wall. It was a perfect space for the breathtaking eighteenth-century tester bed that dominated the room. The ornately carved bed was upholstered in a lapis blue silk damask fabric and accented with gold braided trim and delicate fringe. It was exquisite, and Bree just had to touch it. She caressed the smooth carved post and luxurious fabric. She had never seen such a phenomenal restoration that wasn't in a museum.

"You sleep in this?" Bree was awestruck. "Can I...just see what it's like?" When Bree was younger she remembered wishing she could sneak a nap in one of the beds in the Biltmore. Just so she could see what it was like to live and sleep like a Vanderbilt.

"Absolutely."

She hesitated, as if she were about to break a cardinal rule, before she eased herself up into the bed. She lay on her back and stared up into the canopy. Its tight, flawless pleats emphasized the sharp contours of the canted sides. She imagined the spectacular feeling of running her fingers over the pristine folds. Carson slipped in to the bed beside her. "Carson, this is...I'm speechless."

"Took me years to get it right. At first I thought I was out of my mind for using it, but then I thought, what good is a bed if you can't sleep in it?" Carson rolled over, propped herself up on her elbow, and looked down at Bree. "Or make love in it."

Bree's stomach fluttered and her body burned to life. She stared into Carson's crystal blue eyes and watched them turn steely with desire. When Carson kissed her, the whole world disappeared. They kissed with fervid hunger, and Bree's entire body burned with need. She needed Carson. She needed to feel the searing heat of her skin pressed into hers. Bree rolled Carson to her back and with one hand flicked open each button of her shirt until it fell open at her sides. Bree loved that Carson never wore a bra, as her breasts were small and perfect. She twisted each nipple between her thumb and forefinger until they tightened. Carson's breath hissed through her teeth, and the sound sent a rush of warmth between Bree's legs. She wanted more.

Bree brushed the palm of her hand down Carson's belly to the button of her jeans. She released the button and slipped her hand down into Carson's panties. Carson's hips jerked upward at the contact. Bree wanted to feel Carson move like that under her. She sat up and slid her leg over Carson, and she could feel their heat combine. The seam of her jeans rubbed her clit as she pressed herself down onto Carson. It wasn't enough. Bree needed to feel Carson's skin on hers. She stripped away her shirt and bra and tossed them onto the floor. She slipped off her jeans and panties as Carson also kicked out of her own offending clothes.

Bree leaned over Carson and braced herself up with one arm as she slid the other between them and into the smooth slick folds between Carson's legs. She closed her eyes and reveled in the warm wetness. When Bree applied firm fingers to Carson's clit, she bucked beneath her. It was the reaction she wanted. Bree wanted Carson to come for her. She was wild and desperate as Bree claimed Carson's mouth with her own.

She slipped two fingers into Carson while she circled the firm peak with her thumb. Carson gasped.

"Do you like that?"

"Oh, yes," Carson replied breathlessly. "Please don't stop."

"Not until you come for me," Bree assured her.

Bree pulsed her fingers in and out of Carson, who thrust her hips in rhythm. Bree dipped her head and sucked hard on a nipple.

"Yes!" Carson cried out. "I'm so close, baby."

Bree inserted another finger and pressed deeper. She was close. Bree could feel her begin to tighten around her fingers, and she filled Carson.

"Come for me. I want to feel you in my hand."

Bree quickened her pace as Carson begged. "Please. Oh God. Yes." Carson tightened around Bree's hand, and her entire body jerked and stiffened. Bree stilled her hand and felt the contractions pulse around her fingers. Carson's breath slowed as her body relaxed. Bree laid herself alongside her, content to bask in Carson's afterglow. But Carson had other plans.

Suddenly, Bree was on her back. She watched as Carson kissed and licked her way down over her breasts and stomach before she settled between Bree's legs. Carson looked into Bree's eyes as she stuck out her tongue and flicked Bree's swollen and sensitive clit. Bree's head fell back as Carson took her into her mouth. Bree's hips bucked and jerked as Carson sucked and licked her into a frenzy. Bree didn't have to beg, but she did. She wanted to come for Carson and she was going to. She weaved her fingers through Carson's short hair and pressed herself deeper into her mouth. When Carson slid her finger inside Bree, she went over the edge. Bree's body shuddered, and she cried out in ecstasy before falling limp and satisfied. Carson crawled up to Bree's side and cradled her close against her throbbing body. She held her long after their breathing slowed and pulses returned to normal.

Bree had no idea how long they'd been asleep when her phone rang. She fumbled with her pants to get them to release the phone from the pocket. She looked at the time before she answered her uncle's call. "I'm so sorry. We're leaving now."

"You are lucky you answered on the first ring, young lady."

Bree knew he would have blown up her phone had she not answered, so she was lucky. "We're on our way."

"All right, drive safe, kiddo."

"Busted!" Carson joked as she rolled off the bed and tossed Bree the rest of her clothes.

Bree put her shirt on and reached for her pants. "Whose idea was it to invite them over for dinner and a movie at my place?"

"That was all you, my love," Carson said as she held up Bree's forgotten bra.

CHAPTER TWENTY-SIX

Carson opened her eyes and pulled Bree closer. She sighed in utter contentment. Carson couldn't imagine a better way to wake up in the morning than spooned naked against Bree's sensuous body.

"Good morning," Bree murmured.

Carson hadn't meant to wake her. "I'm sorry for waking you."

"You didn't. I've just been lying here listening to you breathe and thinking about how good you feel in my bed."

"I like how I feel in your bed, especially like this." Carson kissed Bree's neck. "How did you sleep?"

"Perfectly. I don't think I've slept all the way through the night in years." Bree caressed the arms that held her. "I think you were just what I needed."

Carson smiled at the thought of being what Bree needed to be happy. "Are you hungry?"

"For you or for bacon?"

Carson laughed. Bree loved her bacon, and Carson adored her pork addiction. "At the moment I was thinking for bacon, but I could be persuaded."

"Then, yes. First you and then bacon." Bree rolled onto her back and looked at Carson.

"How about this, I'll go down and make breakfast. Then bring it back up here where you can have your bacon and eat it, too." Carson wagged her eyebrows.

Bree chuckled. "I see what you did there. And while it was a terrible pun, it's an excellent idea."

"I tried."

Bree laughed. "Hardly."

"True. But it made you laugh. Stay here, I'll be back." Carson kissed Bree and rolled out of bed. She slipped on a tank top and her pig jammies and trotted downstairs to the kitchen.

Carson gathered the items for pancakes, fried eggs, and of course, bacon and began preparing breakfast for her and Bree. She flipped on the kitchen radio and sang along to the music as she danced in front of the stove. Carson couldn't remember when she had ever woken up with a woman, let alone stayed to make her breakfast. She liked it, a lot. She fantasized about waking up early on the weekends to make breakfast for Bree while she sat at the table sipping her coffee and reading the morning paper. For the first time, Carson could see a piece of her future and it was all about Bree.

As she shimmied to a P!nk song and flipped the bacon, the doorbell rang. She hollered up to Bree, "Don't move. I'll get it."

Bree shouted back, "I'm not. I'm sure it's Jim. He probably smelled the bacon. Tell him he can't have any."

"I will," Carson replied as she opened the door. Bree was right; it was Jim. "Hey, Jimbo. Bree says no bacon for you."

"Well, hey, Car. I didn't see your truck."

"I'm on the bike. It's in the garage in case it rained. Come in."

Jim followed Carson back to the kitchen. "Oh, okay. So, I came to see if Bree wanted to come meet Barb and me for some breakfast and then hit a few of the antique shops. But never mind."

"Oh. Well, I don't know if she had anything planned for today, but she's still in bed. I told her I'd make her bacon and bring it up."

"You've figured out the way to her heart." Jim reached for a piece as Carson laid the crispy strips onto the paper towel–covered plate.

"Ah, Bree said no bacon for you, mister." Carson pointed her spatula at him.

"Aww, how can you deny an old man one little slice of salty heaven?"

"Give me a break. You're in your fifties." Jim pouted his lip at her. "Seriously? Now I know where she gets it from. Although I must say, it's much cuter when she does it." Carson winked. "Take it. But if she asks, I'm telling her you stole it."

Jim stuck the whole piece in his mouth at once. "Can't prove anything without evidence," he said from greasy lips. "Ask Bree if she's interested in antiques. I'll stop back over before I head out." He reached back for the bacon, but Carson jerked the plate away from him.

Jim smiled and patted Carson's cheek. "You're a good kid, Car. And no more stalling, tell her about Dayton." He let himself out and Carson took the food up to Bree.

Bree sat up when she saw Carson come through the door. "How many pieces did he con you out of with his sad puppy-dog pout?"

Carson handed Bree her plate. "Just one, almost two, but I was faster than he was."

"Good thing. He loves bacon more than I do."

"He wanted to know if we wanted to go antiquing with him and Barbara. I told him I didn't know what, if anything, you had planned. He said he'd come back in a little bit."

"I've got nothing planned except finishing this delicious breakfast and then forcing you into taking a long, hot shower with me."

"Oh. Well, I don't think force will be necessary." Carson would've thrown out her breakfast had Bree said she wanted her in the shower right then.

"Good to know."

❖

After they finished eating, Carson got out of bed and gathered the empty plates together. She could've stayed in bed all day with Bree, but she did want a hot shower in every way possible. Carson leaned over Bree, who sat on the edge of the bed. "I'll take these downstairs. You get in that shower and get it warm for me."

"Ooh, yes, ma'am. Anything you say." Bree pulled Carson in close by her shirt. "I don't know how I've lived so long without waking up beside you. There isn't a morning that goes by that I don't want you right here with me, just like this."

Carson took the plates from Bree's hands and set them on the nightstand next to her. She watched as Bree hooked her thumbs under the hem of her tank and slipped her soft hands over her smooth abdomen. Bree pinched one of Carson's bare nipples into a tight bud as she worked the other one to a peak in her mouth. Carson would move heaven and earth to feel Bree's touch every day. But there was something she needed to do in order to make sure in full confidence that her dream would last forever. Carson grabbed Bree's hands and gripped them. "Bree. I have something to tell you."

The look on Bree's face was indescribable. It was awash with fear, anxiety, and surprise. She pulled her hands away and set them in her lap. "What…what is it?"

The trepidation in Bree's face caused Carson to panic. Carson sat down and stared at her beautiful Bree. She was the sweetest, most caring woman Carson had ever met. Even as the pain of losing her hung over her head, she couldn't help but smile at the beauty that was Bree. "You are gorgeous." Carson's heart filled with happiness, but it was followed by a sudden twist of sadness. Carson couldn't have hid her emotions even if she had expected them, and Bree noticed immediately.

Bree stared, her face stricken white with apprehension. "Carson? What's wrong? Please don't say you're leaving me." Bree's smile was forced in an attempt to make the statement a joke.

A knot tied in her throat, and Carson didn't know how to say what she needed to. She was so adept at thinking on her feet even in awkward or uncomfortable situations, yet this time it was beyond her experience. "No. I…When…Okay…" Carson inhaled deeply.

"Carson, you're freaking me out, love. What's wrong?" Bree grabbed Carson's hand and pulled in close. "Look at me."

She called her love, and it wrenched Carson's gut. Carson looked at Bree's warm brown eyes and reached out to her face. "All I want is for you to be happy."

"Oh, Carson, I know. And you make me so happy." Bree leaned in to kiss her, but Carson moved back. Bree looked wounded. "Um, Carson. What is going on? Tell me, now. Please."

"I want you to be happy. I want us to be happy, together. But in order to do that I have to make sure that this is where I need to be."

Bree cut her off. "What the hell are you talking about?"

"I've had a job opportunity come to me. It's sort of a no-brainer. A simple, 'thanks, but no thanks.' But…"

Bree looked shocked but said nothing.

"But then I thought about the future and the regrets and what-ifs."

"Regrets? What-ifs? You mean like 'What if you regret giving up your life and future for me?'" The tears hung in Bree's eyes as she spoke.

"Something like that, I guess." Carson pressed Bree's hand over her heart. "Bree, I know here that this is where I want to be." Her heart broke as she watched the tears streak down Bree's cheeks. "But I need to know in my head, that I'm making the right and rational decision. I would never forgive myself if I hurt you."

"Where is the position?" Bree asked.

"The Dayton Art Institute. I got a recruitment package a couple weeks ago for their new preservation director. I have no idea where they got my name because I know I didn't apply for it."

Bree pulled back her hand and set it in her lap. "When is the interview?" Her voice now void of emotion.

"It's spread out over two days next week. Listen to me, sweetheart." Carson grabbed Bree's hand and kissed her palm. "I told you, I want to be with you. I just have to do this. I'll be back, I promise."

Bree felt the nausea rise up inside her. Bree clutched the sheets to her chest. Bree ripped her hand back and stood up.

"I'm sorry, sweetheart. I didn't mean to keep it from you. I don't want to lose you."

"It's fine." She reached for her robe that hung on the bedpost. She wrapped herself in the robe before she walked toward the door without another word. Carson followed her.

Bree headed down to the kitchen for a drink. She wanted beer or wine, but it wasn't even eleven a.m. She opted for water and sat at the kitchen table without drinking it. Bree pushed her palms into her eyes and rubbed. *I'll be back, I promise.* She stood up from the table and hit her elbow on the glass.

Bree stared as she watched it tumble and shatter on the tile floor. "Son of a bitch!" Bree crouched down to pick up the shards.

"Bree." Carson barreled into the kitchen at the sound of the breaking glass. "Are you okay?"

Bree didn't look up at Carson. "I'm fine. Dropped a glass."

Carson reached down for Bree. "Come sit. I'll get that."

Bree drew back from Carson's touch. "I'm fine. I just need to get the broom and some paper towels."

Carson was taken aback by Bree's snappish withdrawal but retrieved the broom and towels for Bree. As Bree wiped the water from the floor, Carson swept the surrounding area for glass. She waited for Bree to get up before she finished. Carson filled the dustpan with the glass remnants and emptied it into the trash bin. Bree stood at the kitchen sink and stared out the window as the wet towels dripped into the growing puddle on the floor. Carson took them from her hands and set them in the sink, and Bree never moved. "Would you like another glass of water?"

Bree shook her head and walked out of the kitchen. She didn't know where she was headed; she just wandered into the living room. She stood spiritlessly at the base of the staircase.

Carson stood behind her for a moment before she spoke. "Will you talk to me, please? Are you all right?"

Bree wasn't all right, and it was apparent that she didn't want to talk about it. Bree went to the bedroom door and opened it. "I'm fine, Carson. Please, stop asking me," Bree demanded, and Carson looked stunned by her brashness. "I'm sorry. I just…I think maybe I should be alone right now."

"Oh, okay. Well, then I should go. Will you be o—"

Carson stopped mid-sentence when Bree raised her eyebrows as she anticipated the question. "Right. I'm gonna go."

Bree walked Carson downstairs to the garage door and pressed the automatic opener. Sadness and concern covered Carson's face, and it wrenched at Bree's heart. She didn't know what she was doing or why she was sending Carson away. She just didn't know what else to do while she struggled to stop her world as it spiraled out of control.

Carson stood in front of Bree. "I'll call you later?"

Bree responded with a single nod. Carson pulled Bree in close and kissed her on the forehead. Bree said nothing. She stepped back and watched Carson ease the bike out of the garage before she threw her leg over and kicked it to life. Bree lifelessly pressed the button for the door and stared as Carson drove away with her heart.

❖

When Carson pulled out of the driveway, she spotted Jim in the front yard and pulled over onto the shoulder. He walked over to her with a confused expression.

"Where are you going?" Jim asked as he wiped his dirty hands on his jeans.

"Home."

"What? Why?"

"Just giving her some space. I told her about the interview, and to say she doesn't want to talk about it right now is an understatement. She didn't want me there."

"She made you leave? What did she say?"

"There weren't a lot of words, but she's hurt, Jim. Will you please check in on her a few times? I need to know she's okay."

"Absolutely, Car. You go home. I'll call you in a little bit and let you know how she's doing. Okay?" Jim patted Carson on the arm. "Don't worry. She'll be fine, kiddo."

"Thanks. I hope so." Carson started her bike and rode off down the street.

Jim watched Carson leave and then headed up the hill to Bree's house, but there was no answer. He decided to leave her be.

CHAPTER TWENTY-SEVEN

Bree poured the batter onto the hot skillet. She stared at the bubbles that rose and popped on the surface of her dinner-plate-sized pancake. It was just before noon, and Bree was still in her robe. Bree hadn't seen or spoken to Carson since she rode away on her bike days before, but she was all Bree could think about—asleep or awake. She'd called in sick for the first few days of the week in order to avoid the awkwardness of seeing her at work but not knowing what to say. Bree missed Carson more than she wanted to, but she needed time to think.

Things had moved so naturally between them over the last few weeks that Bree never would have expected the bomb that Carson dropped on her, even though she should have. She had spent years building up the protective walls around her heart to ensure she would never again feel the pain of losing someone she cared about. Bree knew it was an irrational precaution, but it made her feel like she had some semblance of control over her heart. Carson had somehow scaled those walls undetected, and it left Bree in the rubble. *I'll be back, I promise.* She'd heard those same words before, and they were a lie. How could she trust that Carson would fulfill the promise that Marion hadn't?

The smell of smoke and a burning pancake jolted Bree

from her mind. She flipped the fan button on her range hood, turned off the burner, and swatted at the smoky air with a dishrag. As she pushed open the French doors onto the patio, her cell phone rang. She continued to fan the smoke outside as she answered the phone. It wasn't until she heard Carson's voice that she realized she should've looked at the caller ID first. Bree had avoided her calls for four days until then, and it was too late to hang up. "Hi."

"Hi. I'm surprised you answered the phone this time. I assumed I'd be leaving another voice mail."

"Yeah. I was sort of distracted when I answered."

"Oh. I see. Thank God for little distractions, then."

"Yeah, just a small kitchen fire is all."

"Shit, Bree are you okay?"

"I'm fine. Just smoke. It's mostly gone now. So, how are things?" She wanted to hear Carson say that the last few days were as bad for her as they had been for Bree. She stepped out onto the back porch and sat on the deck.

"Oh, you know."

"Yeah, I know." Bree swung her legs down over the side and stared at the grass below.

"Bree, I wanted to tell you again that I'm sorry and that I'll be home tonight. Maybe I could come by and we could talk."

Bree's stomach twisted and a lump rose in her throat. She was a mix of anticipation and apprehension. She wanted to see and hold Carson with every fiber of her being, but Bree's heart ached at the thought of what she had to say. "I don't—"

"Please, Bree. I miss you. I'm not going to Ohio. Hell, they probably wouldn't even offer me the job after the fool I made of myself while I was there. But I don't care, because I don't want to be in Dayton. I don't want to be anywhere that doesn't have you. I need you, Bree. I need us. Please."

The tears ran down her cheeks, and Bree did nothing to stop them. She'd thought about that moment every day since she had pushed Carson out of her life. What would she say? What would she do if she had one more chance to tell her how she felt? "Are you really not going?"

"I am most definitely not going, my love. Please, when can I see you?"

Bree's heart burst with joy, and she knew. "Tomorrow morning. Meet me at the staircase at eight."

"Oh, sweetheart, anything. I'll see you tomorrow."

"Tomorrow." Bree forced herself to say good-bye to Carson and hang up the phone.

CHAPTER TWENTY-EIGHT

B ree paced at the base of the staircase. She was both nervous and excited to see Carson. She had spent the previous night pressed into her couch while she scrolled through the pictures on her phone. Each time she came to a photo of Carson, the butterflies in her stomach fluttered, and she couldn't help but smile. Bree couldn't believe that someone could make her feel that way even through pictures. Her favorite was one she took of Carson as she lay in her lap and stuck her tongue out at the camera. It was such a carefree and happy moment that Bree's heart swelled with love.

Bree tried to wait patiently as she had planned, but when her eyes met Carson's from across the room she grew anxious. She tried to contain herself as she shuffled across the foyer to close the immense space between them. The exhaustion she had felt from her days of restless sleep had all but disappeared as her heart raced with anticipation. They each slid to a stop inches from the other. Bree took a few moments to stare into Carson's clear crystal eyes and fell into character. "Good morning, Ms. Harper, and welcome to the Biltmore Estate."

Carson chuckled and played along. "Thank you."

"If you are ready, we can go ahead and get started with your private tour."

Carson raised her eyebrow at Bree. "A private tour?"

"Yes. Just for you. Shall we?" Bree motioned in the direction of the staircase.

❖

Bree walked Carson back toward the staircase, although Carson felt more like she had floated there. Carson didn't care if the tour was for a hundred people. She would never have noticed them anyway. "Yes."

"This is the Grand Staircase. Its cantilevered design uses the weight of the walls to support each limestone step." Bree pointed upward to the massive light fixture. "This seventeen hundred pound electric chandelier contains seventy-two bulbs and is held aloft by a single bolt." She moved up to the second step. "I was standing right here the first moment I saw you. You ran toward me at a sprint. I was so mesmerized by you that I barely jumped out of the way before you ran me over. I watched you take the steps two at a time until you disappeared up there. Follow me, please." Bree led Carson across the foyer to the Winter Garden.

"This garden was often used for family dinners by the Vanderbilts." Bree stood inside one of the small doorways that led into the sunny room. "Each and every morning as I start my tours you stand here and watch me. You think I don't see you, but I do, and it makes me smile."

Carson had been on many tours through the Biltmore, but this was already the one she would always remember. She walked with Bree to the Banquet Hall.

"This is the Banquet Hall and one of my favorite rooms in the house. Up there is the Organ Balcony, which houses a 1916 Skinner Pipe Organ. The organ itself is not original to the house, as the original was donated to a church in the village.

This one was installed in 1999." Bree turned to Carson and addressed her. "You went out of your way to participate in my first tour of the house. You never took your eyes off me, and I was scared to death to screw up in front of you. You made me so nervous that I still don't know how I passed that test. This way, please." Bree led Carson back to the staircase and up to the second floor.

When they entered the Damask Room, Carson knew what was coming. Bree was about to take her opportunity to razz her for the verbal lashing Carson had given her.

"This is the Damask Room. I accidentally touched this chair and set off the alarms." It was all she said before she sped off into the next room. "This is the Claude Room, named after one of Vanderbilt's favorite artists." Bree stopped in the middle of the room. "And here is where I was verbally accosted by the most gorgeous and passionate woman I have ever laid eyes on. You made me so angry and so exhilarated that I didn't know if I wanted to punch you or kiss you." Carson laughed and reached out for Bree. "No, no. Please don't molest the staff... yet." Bree winked.

Carson followed along as Bree led them back downstairs. She was overwhelmed by the pure thoughtfulness and heart that Bree had put into this time together. She didn't think she could love Bree any more than she did after their run-in with Marion, but each minute of the tour made her fall deeper in love with who Bree was. Carson wanted to hold her in her arms and promise her anything she could ever want or need. She would give her every cloud in the sky if she asked for it. She deserved it, and Carson wanted to be the one who gave it to her.

Bree continued out the main entrance and onto the lawn. "This is the Biltmore. It was built over a course of six years and was designed by Richard Morris Hunt and Frederick Law

Olmstead." Bree pointed to the facade of the house. "The building is constructed from Indiana limestone that Vanderbilt specifically chose for its bright and reflective qualities. The roof tiles were attached one at a time by hand, and the copper flashings were installed to keep out moisture." Bree turned and stepped toward Carson. She looked up at Carson and smiled. "It's where I grew up and where everyone I hold dear calls home. It's where I found myself, where I found my future, and most importantly, it's where I fell in love with you."

Bree threw her arms around Carson's shoulders and pulled her close. A knot tied in Carson's throat. She stared into Bree's warm eyes and knew she was in the very place she was meant to be. "I love you so much."

"And I love you, Carson Harper."

"Is it okay if I molest you now?"

Bree flashed a smile before Carson kissed her with all the passion and love that she had ever felt. She was complete, and they were home.

Chapter Twenty-nine

Oh my God. I'm so nervous."

"You're nervous? Imagine how your uncle feels right now." Barbara tucked a wayward strand of hair back behind Bree's ear.

"Can you believe this is finally happening?"

"It's a dream come true." Bree clutched Barbara's hand in hers.

A man in a black tuxedo entered the room and announced that it was time to go. Bree and Barbara giggled like teenagers and squeezed each other's hands. Bree was overwhelmed with emotion. She tipped her head back and took a deep breath.

"Ready?" Barbara asked.

"As I'll ever be." Bree and Barbara followed the gentleman out into the hallway and down the corridor to where the horse-drawn carriage waited. A finely dressed man in a black top hat stood next to a Victorian vis-à-vis carriage drawn by two large draft horses. Bree had never been on this side of the moment, and she was awestruck. The man helped her up. She sat and reached out her hand to steady Barbara as she climbed in across from her.

Once they were settled, the coachman flicked the reins and they were on their way.

Bree's heart raced with excitement and anticipation. She turned to Barbara. "Is this everything you thought it would be?"

"And more. How are you feeling?"

"Still quite nervous, actually. You?"

"Excited." Barbara grinned from ear to ear and reached across to squeeze Bree's knee through her dress.

As they pulled around onto the side road, Bree and Barbara gasped at the sight. The sun was setting over the distant mountains, and the white limestone of the house blushed with pink and yellow. The clouds that billowed in the sky were flushed pink, and Bree was overwhelmed at the happiness that flooded her soul. They pulled to a stop on the lawn where the beginning of a long white aisle was lined with bouquets of fall blooms. Two large cast iron gates weaved with the colors of autumn and vines stood tall to welcome them.

"Here we are. You are so beautiful." Bree stood and took the footman's hand as he helped her down from the carriage. She adjusted her dress before she smiled and stepped purposefully down the aisle toward Carson and her uncle. Rustic lanterns hung from cast iron posts at the end of each row. The candles in each flickered and cast a romantic light on the white fabric at her feet and illuminated the warm hues of the flowers that spiraled up the posts.

Bree approached the large arbor of the altar. Matching blooms and flowers adorned the ornate archway that framed the grand entrance of the beautiful estate behind it. The setting sun glinted off the reflective glass windows and added another level of enchanting light. Carson looked stunning in a black suit and tie. Bree couldn't take her eyes off Carson. As Bree approached the end of the aisle, she winked at her and blew a kiss to Jim. She slipped off to her place on the left and turned as the guests stood to face Barbara in her beautiful white gown.

Bree looked at her uncle as everyone else watched the bride. His expression was one of pure love and true happiness. She knew what it looked like because it was what she felt when she gazed at Carson. Her eyes met Carson's as they looked adoringly back at her. Yes. She knew those feelings so well. Carson smiled and Bree's heart melted. Bree loved her beyond words, and it meant more than anything that Carson stood next to her uncle on his amazing day. Bree smiled and whispered, "Thank you."

And Carson replied as always, "Anything."

About the Author

Tina Michele is a Florida girl living on the banks of the Indian River Lagoon in the biggest small town on the Space Coast. She enjoys all the benefits of living in the Sunshine State. During the day, she pretends to do what they pay her for but really spends most of that time daydreaming and plotting some wild adventure. She graduated from the University of Central Florida with her BA in interdisciplinary studies— the most liberal of the liberal arts degrees—majoring in fine art and writing with a minor in women's studies. To say she is motivated by her Right brain is a major understatement. Afflicted with self-diagnosed Sagittarian Attention Deficit Disorder, she spends a lot of time starting projects that she may, possibly, one day, probably finish. When she isn't writing, playing, drawing, painting, or creating something of some sort, she feeds and waters the three dogs that are permanently tethered to her hindquarters.

Tina can be contacted at tina@tmichele.com or follow her on twitter @tmichelewrites.

Books Available From Bold Strokes Books

The Chameleon's Tale by Andrea Bramhall. Two old friends must work through a web of lies and deceit to find themselves again, but in the search they discover far more than they ever went looking for. (978-1-62639-363-9)

Side Effects by VK Powell. Detective Jordan Bishop and Dr. Neela Sahjani must decide if it's easier to trust someone with your heart or your life as they face threatening protestors, corrupt politicians, and their increasing attraction. (978-1-62639-364-6)

Autumn Spring by Shelley Thrasher. Can Bree and Linda, two women in the autumn of their lives, put their hearts first and find the love they've never dared seize? (978-1-62639-365-3)

Warm November by Kathleen Knowles. What do you do if the one woman you want is the only one you can't have? (978-1-62639-366-0)

In Every Cloud by Tina Michele. When Bree finally leaves her shattered life behind, is she strong enough to salvage the remaining pieces of her heart and find the place where it truly fits? (978-1-62639-413-1)

Rise of the Gorgon by Tanai Walker. When independent Internet journalist Elle Pharell goes to Kuwait to investigate a veteran's mysterious suicide, she hires Cassandra Hunt, an interpreter with a covert agenda. (978-1-62639-367-7)

Crossed by Meredith Doench. Agent Luce Hansen returns home to catch a killer and risks everything to revisit the unsolved murder of her first girlfriend and confront the demons of her youth. (978-1-62639-361-5)

Making a Comeback by Julie Blair. Music and love take center stage when jazz pianist Liz Randall tries to make a comeback with the help of her reclusive, blind neighbor, Jac Winters. (978-1-62639-357-8)

The Price of Honor by Radclyffe. Honor and duty are not always black and white—and when self-styled patriots take up arms against the government, the price of honor may be a life. (978-1-62639-359-2)

Soul Unique by Gun Brooke. Self-proclaimed cynic Greer Landon falls for Hayden Rowe's paintings and the young woman shortly after, but will Hayden, who lives with Asperger syndrome, trust her and reciprocate her feelings? (978-1-62639-358-5)

Mounting Evidence by Karis Walsh. Lieutenant Abigail Hargrove and her mounted police unit need to solve a murder and protect wetland biologist Kira Lovell during the Washington State Fair. (978-1-62639-343-1)

Threads of the Heart by Jeannie Levig. Maggie and Addison Rae-McInnis share a love and a life, but are the threads that bind them together strong enough to withstand Addison's restlessness and the seductive Victoria Fontaine? (978-1-62639-410-0)

Sheltered Love by MJ Williamz. Boone Fairway and Grey Dawson—two women touched by abuse—overcome their pasts to find happiness in each other. (978-1-62639-362-2)

Searching for Celia by Elizabeth Ridley. As American spy novelist Dayle Salvesen investigates the mysterious disappearance of her ex-lover, Celia, in London, she begins questioning how well she knew Celia—and how well she knows herself. (978-1-62639-356-1).

Hardwired by C.P. Rowlands. Award-winning teacher Clary Stone and Leefe Ellis, manager of the homeless shelter for small children, stand together in a part of Clary's hometown that she never knew existed. (978-1-62639-351-6)

The Muse by Meghan O'Brien. Erotica author Kate McMannis struggles with writer's block until a gorgeous muse entices her into a world of fantasy sex and inadvertent romance. (978-1-62639-223-6)

No Good Reason by Cari Hunter. A violent kidnapping in a Peak District village pushes Detective Sanne Jensen and lifelong friend Dr. Meg Fielding closer, just as it threatens to tear everything apart. (978-1-62639-352-3)

Romance by the Book by Jo Victor. If Cam didn't keep disrupting her life, maybe Alex could uncover the secret of a century-old love story, and solve the greatest mystery of all—her own heart. (978-1-62639-353-0)